New York Times bestselling author Anne Perry lives in Portmahomack, Scotland. She writes the Victorian mystery series featuring Thomas and Charlotte Pitt, adapted for television as *The Cater Street Hangman,* and watched by millions of viewers when it was broadcast by ITV. She is also the author of the critically acclaimed William and Hester Monk series, and a quintet of novels set during the First World War.

Praise for Anne Perry's novels:

'A beauty: brilliantly presented, ingeniously developed and packed with political implications that reverberate on every level of British society . . . delivers Perry's most harrowing insights into the secret lives of the elegant Victorians who have long enchanted and repelled her'   *New York Times Book Review*

'The novel has a totally contemporary feel and is admirably well-written'   *Guardian*

'A complex plot supported by superb storytelling'   *Scotland on Sunday*

'Master storyteller Anne Perry moves closer to Dickens as she lifts the lace curtain from Victorian society to reveal its shocking secrets'   Sharyn McCrumb

'Anne ⬛⬛⬛⬛⬛⬛⬛⬛⬛⬛⬛⬛⬛⬛⬛⬛ d story, but almost outdoⷮ   *Northern Echo*

Also by Anne Perry and available from Headline

Tathea
Come Armaggedon
The One Thing More
A Christmas Journey
A Christmas Visitor
A Christmas Guest

World War I series
No Graves as Yet
Shoulder the Sky
Angels in the Gloom
At Some Disputed Barricade
We Shall Not Sleep

The Inspector Pitt series
Bedford Square
Half Moon Street
The Whitechapel Conspiracy
Southampton Row
Seven Dials
Long Spoon Lane

The William Monk series
The Face of a Stranger
A Dangerous Mourning
Defend and Betray
A Sudden, Fearful Death
The Sins of the Wolf
Cain His Brother
Weighed in the Balance
The Silent Cry
The Whited Sepulchres
The Twisted Root
Slaves and Obsession
A Funeral in Blue
Death of a Stranger
The Shifting Tide
Dark Assassin

A CHRISTMAS SECRET

Anne Perry

headline

First published in Great Britain in 2006 by
HEADLINE PUBLISHING GROUP

First published in Great Britain in 2007 by
HEADLINE PUBLISHING GROUP

2

Cataloguing in Publication Data is available
from the British Library

ISBN 978 0 7553 3429 2

Typeset in Times by Palimpsest Book Production Limited,
Grangemouth, Stirlingshire

Printed and bound in Great Britain by
Mackays of Chatham Ltd, Chatham, Kent

Headline's policy is to use papers that are natural, renewable and
recyclable products and made from wood grown in sustainable forests.
The logging and manufacturing processes are expected to conform
to the environmental regulations of the country of origin.

HEADLINE PUBLISHING GROUP
An Hachette Livre Company
338 Euston Road
London NW1 3BH

www.headline.co.uk
www.hodderheadline.com

To all those who would like to start again.

Clarice Corde leaned back in her seat as the train pulled out of the station in a cloud of steam. Smuts flew, and engine roared as it gathered speed. The rain beat against the window and she could barely see the glistening rooftops of London. It was 14 December 1890, ten days before Christmas Eve. She had been married little more than a year, and she was far from used to being a vicar's wife. Neither obedience nor tact came to her except with a considerable effort, but she made it for Dominic's sake.

She glanced sideways at him now and saw him deep in thought. She knew he was concerned for his ability to rise to this opportunity they had been offered so unexpectedly. The elderly Reverend Mr Wynter had taken a richly deserved holiday; therefore his church, in the small village of Cottisham, needed someone to stand in for him to care for his flock over Christmas.

Dominic had seized the chance. He had been a widower who

1

had abandoned a self-indulgent life and embraced the ministry somewhat late. Perhaps no one but Clarice saw beyond his handsome face and ease of manner to the doubts beneath. She loved him the more fiercely because she knew he understood his own weaknesses as well as the power of his dreams.

He looked up and smiled at her. Once again she was warmed by amazement that he should have chosen her: the awkward sister, the one with the tactless tongue and the disastrous sense of humour rather than any of the reliable and more conventional beauties eager for his attention.

This chance to go to Cottisham, in the county of Hertfordshire, was the greatest Christmas gift they could have been given. It was an escape from serving under the Reverend Mr Spindlewood in the bleak area of industrial London to which Dominic had been sent as curate.

How could she reassure him that his new parishioners expected only patience, and that he should be there to listen and comfort, to assure them of the message of Christmas, and peace on earth?

She reached her hand across and touched his arm, tightening her fingers for a moment. 'It will be good,' she said firmly. 'And being in the country will be fun.'

He smiled at her, his dark eyes bright, knowing what she meant to tell him.

The village was indeed beautiful, even though it boasted little more than a wide green with a duck pond and houses all around it. Many of the dwellings were thatched, their bare winter gardens neatly tidied. Perhaps half a dozen narrow roads twisted away into the surrounding woods and the fields beyond. The church was Saxon: slate-roofed, with a square tower rising high against the wind-torn clouds.

The carriage that had brought them from the station drew up in front of the rambling stone vicarage. The driver unloaded their cases on to the gravel, and drove away.

Clarice looked at the closed door, then at the fine Georgian windows. It was a beautiful house, but it seemed oddly blind, as if it were oblivious to their arrival, and they would knock on the oak door in vain. This was to be their home, and Dominic's challenge and opportunity would be to preach and to minister without supervision, or the constant meddling of the Reverend Mr Spindlewood. Clarice knew she must behave with enthusiasm now, whatever doubt or loneliness she felt. That was what faith was about. Anyone can be cheerful when they are fresh and the sun is shining.

She looked at Dominic once, then marched up to the front door and banged briskly with the lion's-head knocker.

There was total silence from inside.

'Stay here with the boxes,' Dominic said quietly. 'I'll go to the nearest house. They must have left the keys with someone.'

But before he could go more than a dozen steps a stout woman, with hair piled up on her head in an untidy knot, came bustling along the road. She struggled to hold a shawl around her shoulders against the wind.

'All right! All right! I'm coming,' she called out. 'No hurry!

It ain't snowin' yet. You must be the Reverend Mr Corde. An' Mrs Corde, I take it?' She stopped in front of them and looked Clarice up and down dubiously. 'I s'pose you know how to care for a house, an' all?' she said in a tone close to accusation. 'I'm Mrs Wellbeloved. I look after the vicar, but I can't do no more for you than a bit o' the heavy work, 'cos I've got family coming for Christmas, an' I need me holiday too. In't good for a body to work all the days o' the year, an' it in't right to expect it.'

'Of course we don't expect it,' Clarice agreed, although she had in fact expected exactly that. 'If you show me where to find everything, and assist with the laundry, I'm sure that will be most satisfactory.'

Mrs Wellbeloved looked more or less mollified. She produced a large key from her pocket, unlocked the door and led the way in.

Clarice followed her, pleasantly surprised by the warmth of the house, even though the vicar had been gone for a couple of days. It smelled of lavender, beeswax and the faint, earthy perfume of chrysanthemums. Everything looked clean: the wooden floor, the hall table, the doors leading off to left and right, the stairs going up towards a wide landing. There was a large vase of branches and leaves of gold and bronze on the floor. For all her lack of grace, Mrs Wellbeloved seemed to be an excellent housekeeper.

'You'll be liking it here,' she said more to Dominic than to Clarice. It sounded something of an order. 'Folks know how to behave decent. Come to church regular and give to the poor.

4

Won't be nothing for you to do but your duty. Just keep it right for the vicar to come back to. I'm sure he's left you a list of them as needs visiting, but if he hasn't, I can tell you.' She opened the sitting-room door to show them a graceful room with a wide fireplace and bay window, and then closed the door again. 'You'll be takin' all services regular,' she went on, walking quickly towards the kitchen. 'An' you won't be wantin' the sexton, but if you do, he's first on the right on the Glebe Road. Gravedigger's two down beyond.'

'Thank you, Mrs Wellbeloved.' Dominic avoided meeting Clarice's eyes, and answered with as straight a face as he could manage.

'I'll be in reg'lar for the heavy stuff, 'ceptin' Christmas Day, an' Boxin' Day, o' course,' Mrs Wellbeloved continued. 'You'll have enough coal an' coke an' likely enough kindlin', but if you haven't you can go walk in the woods an' pick up plenty. Works best of all if you dry it proper first. An' you'll walk Harry too. I can't be doin' that.'

'Harry?' Dominic asked, puzzled.

'Harry.' She looked at him witheringly. 'The dog! Didn't the vicar tell you about Harry? Retriever, he is. Good as gold, if you treat him right. An' Etta. But you don't need to do nothin' for her, 'cept scraps and stuff, an' milk. She'll fend for herself.'

Clarice made a quick guess. 'Etta's a cat?'

Mrs Wellbeloved looked appeased for their ignorance. 'Right good little mouser, she is. Plain as you like, but clever. Capture 'em all in the end.' She said it with satisfaction, as if she identified with the animal, and were in some oblique way describing herself as well.

Clarice could not help smiling. 'Thank you. I am sure we shall get along excellently. Thank you for showing us in. We shall have a cup of tea, and then unpack.'

'There's everything you'll need for today,' Mrs Wellbeloved nodded. 'Game pie in the pantry, an' plenty o' vegetables, such as there is this time o' year. You'll need onions. Vicar loved 'em. Hot onion soup best thing in the world for a cold, he said. Smells worse 'n whisky, but at least you're sober.' She gave Dominic a hard, level look.

He returned it unflinchingly, and then slowly smiled.

Mrs Wellbeloved grunted, then a pink blush spread up her face and she turned away. 'Handsome is as handsome does,' she muttered under her breath.

Clarice thanked her again and saw her to the door. She was ready to be alone in her new, temporary home, and take stock of things. But first she wanted a cup of tea. It had been a long journey and it was close to the shortest day in the year. Storm clouds were looming up over the trees and the light was fading.

The house was everything she could have hoped. It had charm and individuality. The furniture was all well used, but also well cared for. Nothing really matched, as if each had been gathered as opportunity arose, and yet nothing appeared to be out of place. Oak, mahogany and walnut jostled together, and age had mellowed them all. Elizabethan carving did not clash with Georgian simplicity. Everything seemed to be useful, except for one small table with barley-twist legs, which was there, Clarice guessed, simply because it was liked.

The pictures on the walls were also obviously personal choice: a watercolour of Bamburgh Castle on the Northumberland coast, rising out of the pale sands with the North Sea beyond; a Dutch scene of fishing boats; half a dozen pencil sketches of bare trees; more winter fields and trees in pen and ink. She found them remarkably restful; her eye returned to them again and again. Upstairs she found another sketch, this time of the ruins of Rievaulx Abbey, bare columns and broken walls towering against the clouds.

'Look at this,' she called to Dominic, who was carrying the last case up to the boxroom. 'Isn't it lovely?'

He put the case away before coming to stand a little behind her, his arm around her shoulder. 'Yes,' he agreed, examining the picture carefully. 'I like it very much.' He peered at the signature. 'It's his own! Did you see that?'

'His own?' she asked.

'The bishop told me he painted,' he replied. 'He didn't say how good he was, though. That has both power and grace to it. At least I think so. I'm looking forward to meeting him, when he comes back.'

Clarice caught the edge of ruefulness in his voice. Those three weeks would go by too quickly, and then they would have to return to London, and Mr Spindlewood. Before that time Dominic must somehow show that he was wise enough, gentle enough, and patient in listening to care for the village alone.

He must be passionate and original in his sermons, not only to hold interest but to feed the heart with the special message of Christmas. She knew this mattered to him intensely, and that his belief in himself wavered. Only the total upheaval of his life had made him consider religious faith at all.

She also knew that empty words of assurance from her would not help. He already knew she believed in him, and took it for granted that it was born of her love more than any realism.

'I wonder if he'll do any more drawing while he's away this time,' she said. 'I don't even know where he's gone.'

Clarice awoke the next morning to stand shivering in her night-gown and drew the curtains open on to a glistening white world. The vicarage garden was surprisingly large and backed on to the woods. The trees were dusted with snow in wildly intricate patterns like heavy lace against a lead-grey sky, and the pale light gave it an eerie, luminous quality. She breathed out slowly in amazement at its beauty, momentarily forgetting to shiver.

She stared at it in rapture until suddenly she remembered there was housework to be done: grates to clean out, fires to be laid and lit and breakfast to be cooked. And, of course, Harry and Etta to be fed. She could not afford to wait for Mrs Wellbeloved to come.

A little after ten o'clock, when Dominic was in the study reading some of the vicar's notes and trying to familiarise himself with the parish, there was a noise outside on the gravel drive. Harry came trotting out of the kitchen where he had been asleep by the stove. His nose was in the air and his plumed tail was waving; however, he did not bark.

Clarice snatched her apron off and went to open the door just as the knocker sounded. She pulled it wide to see a man standing just back from the step. He was a little above average height and apparently slender, although under the weight of his winter coat it was hard to tell. His face was fine-boned, not exactly handsome, but full of intelligence and a wry wit. His complexion was deep olive and his eyes had the liquid darkness that comes from the East. However, when he spoke his voice was as English as her own.

'How do you do, Mrs Corde? I am Peter Connaught.' He gestured vaguely behind him. 'From the manor house. I wanted to welcome you to the village.' He held out his hand, then glanced at the smooth, leather glove and apologised, pulling it off.

'How do you do, Mr Connaught?' she replied, smiling at him. 'That is most kind of you. May I offer you a cup of tea? It's terribly cold this morning.'

'That would be most welcome,' he accepted. 'I think it's going to be a hard Christmas – for weather, but I hope not for anything else.'

She stepped back and opened the door wider for him. He came in, glancing around as if perhaps the vicarage might have changed since he had been there last. Then he relaxed and smiled again, reassured. Did he think they would have moved things in a night?

She took his coat, and then showed him into the sitting room, grateful she had lit the fire early and it was pleasantly warm. She noticed how again he looked around, smiling at familiar things, the pictures, the way the furniture was arranged, the worn chairs with their colours blending.

'If you will excuse me, I shall tell my husband you are here. Then I shall bring tea.'

'Of course.' He inclined his head, rubbing his hands together. His polished boots were wet from the snow and the wind had whipped colour into his face.

She went to the study first and opened the door without knocking.

'Dominic, Mr Connaught from the manor house is in the sitting room. I'm just going to bring tea. It's very good of him to come, isn't it?'

He looked a little surprised. 'Yes. And very quick.' There was a note of apprehension in his voice.

Clarice heard it and was afraid he was anxious already that she might be too frank in her opinions, too quick not only to see a better way of doing something, but to say so. It had been known to happen before.

'I suppose I should call upon his wife. She will know all the women in the village and everything about them. He hasn't mentioned her,' she added, biting her lip and looking straight into his eyes. 'But I promise I shall behave perfectly. I will find her delightful and extremely competent, I promise you. Even if she is a blithering idiot with a tongue like a dose of vinegar! I really do promise.'

He stood up. 'Just don't expect me to watch you, and keep a straight face!' he warned, touching her cheek so lightly she barely felt it. 'Don't change too much! I wouldn't care to be Archbishop of Canterbury if I had to lose the person you are in order to do it!'

'Oh, if you were Archbishop of Canterbury,' she said cheerfully, 'I would probably say whatever I pleased! Everyone would be far too in awe of you to criticise me.'

He rolled his eyes, and went out to meet their guest.

Clarice went into the kitchen happily. To be loved for herself, with all her dreams and vulnerabilities, the mistakes and the virtues, was the highest prize in life, and she knew that.

When she returned with the tray of tea and biscuits she found both men seated by the fire talking. They rose immediately and Dominic took the tray from her and set it down. They exchanged the usual pleasantries. She poured and passed Connaught his cup, then Dominic.

'Sir Peter has been telling me a little about the village,' Dominic said, catching her eye. 'His family has been here for centuries.'

She felt herself blush. She had not known his title and had called him 'Mister' when she had asked him in. She wondered if he were offended. Normally she would not have cared, but all this mattered so much. She was not impressed with people's ancestors, but this was not the time to say so. She composed her face into an expression of interest. 'Really? How fortunate you are to have deep roots in such a lovely place.'

'Yes,' he agreed quickly. 'It gives me a great sense of

belonging. And like all privileges, it carries certain obligations. But I believe they are a pleasure also. I was very sad when I learned that Mr Wynter was taking his holiday over Christmas, but now that we have you here, I am sure it will be as excellent as always. Christmas is a great time for healing rifts, forgiving mistakes, and welcoming wanderers home.'

'How very well you express it,' Dominic responded. 'Is that what Mr Wynter has said in the past, or your own feeling?'

Sir Peter looked slightly surprised, even momentarily disconcerted. 'My own. Why do you ask?'

'I thought it was so well phrased I might ask you if I could use it,' Dominic replied candidly. 'I would like to say something truly appropriate in my Watch Night sermon, which has to be as short as possible, yet still to have meaning. But I cannot prepare it until I have at least a slight acquaintance with the village, and the people.'

Sir Peter leaned forward a little, a very slight frown between his dark brows. 'Did Mr Wynter not tell you at least a little about us, collectively and individually?'

Watching him, Clarice had the sudden certainty that the answer mattered to him far more than he wished them to know. There was a tension in the lines of his body, and the knuckles of his beautiful hands were white on his lap.

Dominic appeared not to have noticed. 'Unfortunately I never met him,' he answered. 'The request to fill this post came to me through the Bishop. I gather Mr Wynter's decision to take a holiday was made very quickly.'

'I see.' Sir Peter leaned back again and picked up his tea. 'That is a trifle awkward for you. Whatever I can do I shall be more than happy to. Call upon me at any time. Perhaps you will dine with me at the manor one evening, when you are settled in?' He looked at Clarice. 'I regret my hospitality will offer you no female company, since my mother has passed away, and I am not married, but I promise to show you much that is of interest, if you care for history, art or architecture. I can tell you stories of all manner of people good and evil, tragic and amusing, belonging to this village down the ages.'

She did not have to pretend interest. 'I think that would be infinitely more fun than any feminine gossip I can imagine,' she replied. 'And I will most certainly come.'

He looked pleased, as if the prospect excited him. Obviously he was enormously proud of his heritage and loved to share it, to entertain people, fill them with laughter and a little awe as well. He looked at Dominic. 'I see you have moved the chess-board. You do not play?'

Dominic glanced around. He clearly had no idea where the chessboard had been.

'You didn't?' Sir Peter said quickly. 'It was already gone when you came?'

'Yes. I haven't seen one.' He looked at Clarice questioningly.

'I haven't seen it either,' she said. 'Used Mr Wynter to play?'

A look of pain burned deep in Sir Peter's eyes, then with an effort he banished it. He swallowed the last of his tea. 'Yes. Yes, at one time. He had a particularly beautiful set. Not black and white so much as black and gold. The black was ebony, and the gold that extraordinary shade that yew wood sometimes achieves, almost metallic. Quite beautiful. Still . . .' He rose to his feet. 'It hardly matters. I just noticed because it was such a feature in the room. The light caught it, you know?'

'It sounds wonderful,' Clarice responded, because the silence demanded it, but her mind was filled with the certainty that his reason for asking was nothing like as casual as he had said. There was a depth of emotion in him that could not be explained by the mere absence of an artefact of beauty. What more had it meant to him, and why did he conceal it?

She still wondered as she also rose to her feet and followed him to the door, thanking him again for his kindness in coming.

Mrs Wellbeloved arrived after luncheon, carrying a large bag of potatoes, which she set down on the kitchen table with a grunt of relief. 'You'll be needin' 'em,' she said.

'Thank you,' Clarice accepted, telling herself that Mrs Wellbeloved meant it kindly and it would be most ungracious to tell her that she would rather have gone to the village shop and bought them herself. Three weeks was such a short time to get to know people so she could help Dominic. 'Thank you,' she repeated. 'That was very thoughtful. We had a visitor this morning.' She carried the potatoes into the scullery, followed hopefully by the dog, who was ever optimistic about something new to eat.

'Come down here, did he?' Mrs Wellbeloved said, her eyes

wide with interest. 'Well I never.' She picked up the long-handled broom and began to sweep the kitchen floor.

Clarice returned to the kitchen, Harry still on her heels.

'He said his family has been in the village for years,' she added, tidying one of the cupboards and setting jams, pickles, savoury jelly in some sort of order.

'Years!' Mrs Wellbeloved exclaimed. 'I should say centuries, more like. Since the Normans came, the way he tells it.'

'The Normans! Really?'

'Yes – 1066, you know?' Mrs Wellbeloved looked at her sceptically. How could she be the lady she pretended if she did not know that?

Clarice was amazed. 'That's terribly impressive!'

'Oh, he's impressed.' Mrs Wellbeloved bent awkwardly and picked up the modicum of dust from the floor, carefully pushing it into the dustpan. 'Come over with William the Conqueror, so he said, an' bin in this village since 1200. Everyone knows that.' She made an expression of disdain, then concealed it quickly, reaching for the bucket, putting it in the low, stone sink and turning on the tap.

'He didn't tell me that.' Clarice felt a need to defend him, although she had no idea why.

'Well, there's a surprise then.' Mrs Wellbeloved turned off the tap and heaved the bucket out. She looked at the floor sceptically. 'Don't seem too bad.'

'It isn't,' Clarice retorted. 'We haven't been here a whole day yet. I really don't think you need to do it.'

'P'raps you're right. I'll just do the table then. Got to keep the table clean.' She took the scrubbing brush off its rack, and a large box of yellow kitchen soap. 'Knew his father, Sir Thomas – he was a real gentleman, poor man.'

'Why? What happened to him?'

'Went abroad, he did.' Mrs Wellbeloved began scrubbing energetically, slopping water all over the place, wetting the entire surface of the table at once. 'Foreign parts somewhere out east. Don't recall if he ever said where, exact. Fell in love and married. Then she died, when Sir Peter was only about five or six years old. Wonderful woman, she was, from all he says, an' very beautiful. Sir Thomas were so cut up by it he came home and never went back there, ever. Raised Peter himself, teaching him all about his family, the land, an' all that. Very close, but never got over her death. I s'pose Sir Peter didn't either. He never married.'

'There's time yet,' Clarice said quickly. 'He looks no more than in his forties. He'll want to keep the line going, the family, surely?'

Mrs Wellbeloved put her weight into the scrubbing, her lips tight, soapsuds flying. She stepped sideways and nearly fell over the dog. 'It's his duty,' she agreed. 'But he isn't doing it, for all that. Maybe that's what it was all about.'

'What what was all about?' Clarice asked unashamedly.

'Used to come here often,' Mrs Wellbeloved replied, wringing out a cloth with powerful, red-knuckled hands. 'Twice a week, most months. Played chess with the vicar reg'lar. Loved their game, they did. Then he stopped all of a sudden, about two years ago. Never came here since, except it were business, or with other folk. Vicar never said why, but then he wouldn't. Could keep other folk's secrets better than the grave, he could.'

'You mean they quarrelled?' Clarice felt a stab of disappointment. It seemed such a sad and stupid thing to do. 'What quarrel could be so bad, and last so long?'

Mrs Wellbeloved jerked upright, banging her elbow on the bucket, which was still on the table. She winced. 'Well, it wouldn't be Mr Wynter's fault, an' that's for certain. He was the best man that ever lived in the village, whether his family went back to the manor or the workhouse! Forgive anybody anything, he would, if it were against himself. Tried over and over to make it up with Sir Peter, but Sir Peter weren't having any of it.' She grunted fiercely. 'But the vicar would never say a thing were right if it weren't. Fear o' God were in him like a great light, it was. Mr Corde's a very lucky man to be allowed to step in for him over Christmas.' She nodded several times. 'Walk a few miles in the Reverend's footsteps an' he'll be the better man for it, mark my words.' She wiped half the table dry savagely, lifted the bucket on to the floor, and wiped the other half, wringing the cloth out several times.

Clarice felt defensive of Dominic, but bit her tongue rather than say anything. She took a deep breath. She needed Mrs Wellbeloved on their side. 'He seems to be a very remarkable man, even for a vicar,' she said with as much humility as she could manage.

Mrs Wellbeloved's blunt face softened. 'That he is,' she agreed more gently. 'Man of God, I say. He deserves a holiday. Go off an' do more of his paintings an' drawings, that's what he needs.' She looked Clarice up and down, and then turned away so her face was out of sight. 'Obliged you could come.' She sniffed, choking off the emotion in her voice. She picked up the bucket and threw the dirty water into the sink so hard it splashed up and a good deal of it went out again on either side, waking the cat, who shook herself angrily and curled up again.

Clarice considered whether to wipe the water up for Mrs Wellbeloved, and decided against it. Better to pretend she had not noticed. Instead she fetched Etta a dry towel for her bed and put the kettle on for another cup of tea, and then went to dust the hall – not that it needed it.

There was a sharp drop in the temperature that evening and another heavy fall of snow. Dominic banked the fires high, hoping they would stay burning most of the night, and there would at least be some warmth left in the air by morning.

Dominic looked out of his study window and saw the bleak beauty of the pale light, but he also knew it meant that no one could plough through the deep drifts to leave the village, and there would be some who would find it hard even to leave their homes to fetch food. This was where his ministry could begin. However, he had no knowledge yet at which houses he would be welcome, and he could not afford even one mistake. He was an outsider; temporarily taking the place of a man he realised was deeply loved.

So far he had only one source of information, Mrs Wellbeloved. Clarice's exact words had been, 'She has opinions about everything, which she'll share at the drop of a hat. Be busy about something else, and even if she's talking complete nonsense, for heaven's sake don't argue with her. Local knowledge is her great achievement.'

Clarice was probably right. Dominic had not had to deal with maids before, and had never considered them.

It was time he did so. He rose and went to find Clarice, who was busy in the kitchen warming two flat irons on the top of the range, ready to iron his shirts, which she had washed the day before. Cat and dog were squashed into one basket together by the stove. Dominic looked at Clarice with a deep stab of guilt. She was not beautiful in the traditional way, except for her eyes. There was far too much character in her face, too much readiness to laugh, or to lose her temper. He could not count the times she had embarrassed him. But she was also generous, and swift to forgive. She was without arrogance, and he had never known her make a promise and fail to keep it.

She could have married a man able to give her a large house and maids to look after her every need. She could have had a carriage, fashionable clothes, and invitations in society. Could she really be as happy as she seemed, face flushed, apron around her waist, testing the flat irons for temperature?

She looked up at him and smiled.

'I'm going to see Mrs Wellbeloved,' Dominic told her. 'I need her advice as to who I should call on in this weather. She'll know.'

'Excellent idea,' she approved. Then she frowned. 'Do be tactful with her, won't you She's a funny creature.'

He bit his lip to keep from laughing. 'I had noticed that, my dear.'

'Wrap up well,' she advised. 'It's bitter outside.'

'I'd noticed that too.' He kissed her quickly on the cheek, and then, before she could catch his arm, he turned and went into the hall.

He put a thick, woollen scarf around his neck, then his over-coat, gloves, and a hat. Even so he was still unprepared for the blast of cold as he opened the front door. Instead of a chill in the air as yesterday, there was a slicing wind with the cruel edge of ice on it, and the glare of light off the snow caused him to narrow his eyes. He stepped out and heard the crunch of his own footsteps. It would be very nice to change his mind and go back inside, but he could not afford to. Part of being a vicar was in not making mistakes, not listening to the tempting little voice that told you another day would do, or that there was somebody else to perform the task. He was the man people looked to here to do the work of God, and he must not fail.

He crossed the village green, seeing only a few other foot-prints in the thin, hard snow. The pond was partially iced over, the bench beside it deserted. The air was grey. The houses huddled down, roofs pale; thin trails of smoke smeared up against the sky. Only the blacksmith's forge glowing red looked inviting. Beyond the village, the woods were tangled branches of black, here and there denser where the evergreens clustered, pale-patched where the snow clung.

He passed an old woman with a bundle of sticks and called 'good morning' to her, but her reply was mumbled and he could not make out her words. He increased his pace and finally felt the warmth return to his body, even though his feet were numb, and he could not feel anything in his fingers but the ache of the cold.

Ten minutes later he was knocking on Mrs Wellbeloved's door, and was relieved when she opened it and invited him in. He stepped over the threshold into a dark, warm hallway smelling of floor polish and smoke.

'Well now, Mr Corde,' she said briskly. She refused to call him 'vicar'. 'What can I do for you? 'Fraid you'll have to manage the housework yourselves today. Got company coming, like I said.'

'I need your advice, Mrs Wellbeloved,' he replied, watching her expression change immediately and guarding himself from smiling.

'Ah, well that I can do, Mr Corde.' She smoothed her apron over her hips. 'What is it you need to know? Come in an' sit a moment; it's my duty to spare you that long.' She led the way into a neat front parlour where a fire was just beginning to burn up, and Mr Wellbeloved, a sturdy man with a weathered face and a shock of grey hair, was sitting whittling a piece of wood into a whistle. There was a pile of shavings on a piece of brown paper on the floor in front of him. Painted blocks were neatly stacked beside him.

When introductions were made, and he had explained that he was carving Christmas presents for the grandchildren, Dominic asked Mrs Wellbeloved for advice about whom he should visit. He wrote down her answers, with addresses, in the notebook he had brought with him.

'An' you'd best ask Mr Boscombe to add to that,' her husband put in helpfully. 'Lives at the end o' the lane as you come in from the south. A big house with three gables. He was Vicar's right hand till about six months ago. Knew everything there was, he did.'

Mrs Wellbeloved nodded her agreement. 'That he did, an' all. Good man, Mr Boscombe. He'll see you right.'

'Until about six months ago?' Dominic questioned.

Mr Wellbeloved glared at his wife, then back at Dominic, his knife stopped in mid-air. 'That's right.'

'What happened then?'

Again they looked at each other.

'Don't know,' Mrs Wellbeloved answered. 'That'd be between Mr Boscombe and the vicar. Give up all his church duties, he did. But still a good man, an' very friendly. Nothing whatever you could take against. You go ask him. He'll tell you all as I can't.'

And Dominic had to be content with that. He thanked them and made his way reluctantly out into the bitter air again. With the directions they had given him he walked briskly the half-mile against the wind to the large, thatched house where John and Genevieve Boscombe lived with their four children.

He was welcomed in shyly, but with a gentle warmth that made him immediately comfortable. John Boscombe was a lean, quietly spoken man, with fair hair. Which was thinning a little. His wife was unusually pretty. Her skin was without blemish, her smile quick, and the fact that she was a little plump and her hair was definitely untidy seemed only to add to a sense of warmth.

Dominic heard happy laughter from upstairs, and at least three sets of feet running around. A large dog of indeterminate breed was lying on the floor in the kitchen in front of the range, and the whole room smelled of baking bread and clean linen. There was a pile of sewing in a basket, amongst which there was a bodice of a doll's dress.

'What can we do for you, Vicar?' Boscombe asked. 'A cup of tea for a start? It's turned cold enough to freeze the—' He stopped, colouring faintly at a sharp look from his wife. 'Tea?' he repeated, his blue eyes wide.

'Thank you very much,' Dominic accepted.

Genevieve hastily moved a pile of folded laundry from one of the chairs and invited him to sit down at the kitchen table. He did not need the explanation that this was the only warm room in the house. People careful with money did not burn more fires than they had to. He knew that with sharp familiarity.

There was the sound of a shriek and then giggles from upstairs.

'I need your advice,' he said frankly. 'Mrs Wellbeloved tells me you were very close to the vicar and could advise me as to all the people I should keep a special care for: those alone, unwell, in hard or unhappy circumstances of any kind. I'm not asking for any confidences,' he added quickly, seeing the look of anxiety in Boscombe's face. 'Only where I should begin, and whom I must not overlook.'

Boscombe frowned. 'Did the vicar not tell you those things?'

At the range, Genevieve turned to look at him, the kettle still in her hand.

'No,' Dominic said regretfully. 'I never actually met him. I was directed here by the bishop. I assume Mr Wynter advised him rather late. Perhaps his need to take a holiday arose very suddenly – a relative ill or in need? I was given no details. I was happy to come.'

'Oh!' Boscombe looked surprised, and oddly relieved. 'That was very good of you,' he added hastily. 'Yes, of course we'll both do anything we can to help.'

'Thank you. I'd like to talk to you a little about the vicar's sermons, particularly past Christmases. I don't want to repeat his words, or his exact message, but I'd like to be . . .' Suddenly he was uncertain exactly what he meant. Familiar, but original? Encouraging and new, but not disturbing? That was nonsense. He needed to make up his mind, decide between the safe and the daring. Was Christmas supposed to be safe, comfortable? Nothing more than the restating of old beliefs?

'Yes?' Boscombe prompted.

Dominic smiled self-consciously. 'Appropriate.' This short time in Cottisham mattered so much, and he was making a mess of it, being trite.

Boscombe seemed to relax. 'Of course. Anything I can tell you. But I haven't been … in the vicar's confidence for the last few months. At least, not as closely as I used to be. But I'm sure I can help. What advice did Mrs Wellbeloved give you? I'll see what I can add. I've been here a while, and Genevieve was born here.'

And indeed he did, giving Dominic the colour and flavour of the village life, and in particular those who might have a need – or the reverse; be willing and able to help. He spoke of them all with kindness, but a clear-eyed view of their vulnerabilities. He also summarised several of the vicar's more notable sermons, so Dominic could be aware of their nature.

But when Dominic sat beside his own fire with Clarice that evening, hearing the wind moan in the eaves, rising shrill and more insistent, and Harry snoring gently next to the hearth, it was Boscombe's anxiety that came to his mind. He tried to explain it to her, but put into words it sounded so insubstantial – a matter of hesitations that could as easily have been shyness, or even a matter of discretion – that he felt foolish to have remembered it at all.

He asked after her day: how she was finding the house, and if the work were onerous. He knew she would say it was not, whatever the truth of it. He admired her for that, and was grateful, but it only increased his sense of guilt that he could not give her the standard of comfort she had been used to before they were married.

'Oh, very good,' she said wearily. 'It's a lovely house.' She drew in her breath to add something, then changed her mind. He knew what she had been going to say – that she wished they could stay there. It was far nicer than the grim accommodation they had in London. Of course, Spindlewood and his wife had the vicarage. In the back of Dominic's mind he was always aware of how callous he had been to his first wife in the long past. He had not thought of it as a betrayal at the time, but it had been, deeply and bitterly so. Perhaps if he had been loyal to her, with or without love, she would not have been murdered.

He did not deserve such a second chance. Looking at Clarice sitting in the chair opposite him, the cat in her lap, her face grave, he was overwhelmed with gratitude.

'Except for Harry,' she said, still answering his question. 'He's fine now, but he's been sulking on the back doorstep half the day.'

'Perhaps he wanted to go out.' He started to rise to his feet.

'No, he didn't! I know enough to let a dog out now and then,' she protested. 'He'd only just come in. He sat there most of the time, or wandered around the kitchen pawing at the doors, all of them, even cupboards.'

'Could he have been hungry?' he suggested.

'Dominic! I fed him. He tries the hall cupboard and the cellar, not just the cupboards with food in. I think he really misses the vicar.'

He sat back in his chair again. 'I suppose so. I expect he'll settle. The cat's certainly happy.'

She gave him a quick smile, stroking Etta, who needled her lap happily with her claws, then went back to sleep.

Dominic leaned forward and poked the fire, sending sparks up the chimney. Clarice was right – it was a lovely house. There was almost a familiarity about it, as if at some far distant time he had lived here before and he would know instinctively where everything was. It was like coming home to some origin so far back you had forgotten you belonged here.

The third morning it was even colder. Clarice could see the village pond from the front door when Dominic went out to begin his visiting. The surface was icing over and a dusting of white snow made most of it indistinguishable from the banks. Harry went charging out into it, and had to be brought back, his chest and tummy caked with snow, and then dried off in front of the kitchen stove, loving the attention.

Clarice did not expect Mrs Wellbeloved today, and after feeding Harry and Etta, she set about the sweeping and dusting straight away, as much to keep warm and busy as for any need for it to be done. The sitting-room fire would have to be cleaned out and relit, of course, but since the ashes were still warm, it would be foolish to remove them before time. It was a waste of coal to light it simply for herself, when she could perfectly easily sit in the kitchen.

One day soon she would have to clean out the kitchen stove completely, polish the steels with emery paper, Bath brick and paraffin, black lead the iron parts and then polish them, then wash and whiten the hearthstone. But it did not have to be today. Such a job should really be begun at six in the morning, so she could get the stove set and relit in time for breakfast.

She was still thinking about it with dislike when the doorbell jangled and she went out into the hall to answer it.

A woman was standing on the step. She was muffled in a heavy cloak and had a shawl over her head, but from what Clarice could see of her, she had a handsome face and wide brown eyes, a short upper lip and round chin with extraordinary strength.

'Mrs Corde?' she enquired. She had a pleasant voice, but not the local accent.

'Yes. May I help you?'

'I rather thought I might help you,' the woman replied. 'My name is Mrs Paget. I know Mr Wynter, and I know the village quite well. I imagine many people are willing to do all they can, especially at Christmas, but you might not know who is good at which things: flowers, baking and so on.'

'Oh, thank you,' Clarice said gratefully. 'Please come in. I would be most obliged for any advice at all.' She held the door open wide.

Mrs Paget stepped in as if it were all very familiar, and Clarice had the sudden feeling that perhaps she had been here many times. Possibly since John Boscombe had withdrawn from his church duties she had, in some practical ways, taken over.

Clarice led the way to the kitchen, explaining that she had

not lit the sitting-room fire yet, and offered a cup of tea. Etta bristled at the intrusion and shot past Clarice and up the stairs. Mrs Paget gave a little cry of surprise.

'I'm sorry,' Clarice apologised. 'She's a very odd cat. I think both animals miss Mr Wynter. The dog is in and out like a fiddler's elbow, and nothing seems to satisfy the cat. I've fed her, given her milk, a warm place to lie, but she just sits there like an owl.'

'I'm afraid I don't know animals very well.' Mrs Paget arranged herself on one of the hard-backed chairs by the table, adjusting her skirts. 'I can't offer any advice. I expect you are correct and they are missing Mr Wynter. He is a wonderful man, very charming and utterly trustworthy. He knows everybody's secrets, all their private doubts and griefs, and never whispers a word to anyone. I am happy to help him in any way I can, but even to me he never gives so much as a hint of what needed to be private.'

'Admirable,' Clarice agreed, filling the kettle and setting it on the hob. 'And absolutely necessary. All I really would like to know is who is gifted at what practical skill – and of course who is not!' She gave Mrs Paget a quick smile.

'Oh, quite!' Mrs Paget eased quickly, sinking back with a flash of understanding. 'That can be every bit as much a disaster. At all costs avoid Mrs Lampeter's baking, and Mrs Porter's soup! Never give Mrs Unsworth the flowers. She only has to touch lilies and they go brown.'

They both laughed, and settled to discuss matters of skill,

tact, need and general usefulness. Harry remained sulking in the corner, and Etta never reappeared.

Dominic returned for luncheon, and went out again. Clarice spent the afternoon going through various cupboards, seeing what polishes, brushes and so on she could find, and if she could repack them a little more tidily so as to make more room. It was annoying to open a cupboard door and have the contents slide out around your feet, or worse, fall on top of you from the shelf above.

In the middle of the afternoon she cleaned out and lit the fire in the sitting room to be warm when Dominic came home. He was bound to be frozen. Earlier she had made hot soup – better, she hoped, that Mrs Porter's!

She was tidying the bookshelves behind the sofa in the sitting room when she came across a leather-bound Bible. Its pages were gold-edged, but very well used, as if it were someone's personal possession, rather than one for general reference. She opened it and saw the vicar's name in it on the front page, and dated some fifty years ago. She ruffled the pages, and saw tiny handwritten notes in the margins, particularly in the Book of Isaiah, and in the four Gospels of the New Testament. She had to carry them to the window for enough light to read them. They were very personal. There was a passion and an honesty in them that made her stop reading. They were too intimate; a man's reminder to himself, not to others.

She stood in the fading winter sun, the light greying outside, the fire burning up behind her. Why had he not taken this with him? An accidental omission, surely? It did not belong in this room: in his bedroom, if not with him. He must have left it out to pack, and somehow overlooked it.

She should find his address and send it on to him. The postal service was good; it would get to him in a day or two at the outside. Her mind made up, she went into the study, and looked for the address of Mr Wynter's holiday dwelling. It took her only ten minutes. She was surprised: it was an area of Norfolk she knew quite well, with beautiful wide skies and open beaches facing the North Sea. It would be a wonderful place for him to create more of his pictures. It was famous for its artists. She smiled, imagining him drinking in its splendour, and then striving to capture it on paper.

Then she read the address again. It was a small hotel in one of the seaside villages. But she had been there herself two years ago – and the hotel was closed, turned into a private house. He could not be there. It must be a mistake, an address from a previous holiday – although she had seen no pictures in the house that could be from that region. She would have to put on her coat and boots and go and ask Mrs Wellbeloved. No doubt she would have the correct address. She must send him his scriptures.

But Mrs Wellbeloved had no idea where the vicar was, if he were not at that hotel. She was very sorry, and not a little annoyed also to have been misled. Clarice should try Sir Peter, who might know on account of church business. She could think of no one else.

The light was waning in the winter dusk, but to the north-west the cloud had cleared. As she approached the manor house the sun burned low and spread a tide of scarlet across the snow. She came to the gates: formal wrought iron between magnificent gate quoins with heraldic griffins on each. She tried them and they opened easily. She walked up the curved gravel driveway until she came around the clipped trees and saw the magnificent façade of the early Tudor house, with its mullioned windows and cloistered chimneys. The gardens were formal: space for herbs and flowers between low hedges carefully nurtured into the complicated patterns of an Elizabethan knot garden. I bet there's a maze somewhere to the back, she thought, beyond the old cedars at the side, and the oaks.

She felt a little presumptuous walking up and knocking on the front door uninvited, but her reason was compelling. The Reverend Mr Wynter would need his Bible, his own copy: not something lent to him by a stranger but something with his passions, his dreams and his understandings written in over the years.

She knocked and waited. The purple cloud banners were a pall over the embers of the setting sun. Nothing happened. Then in the fast-fading light she noticed a griffin's head to one side of the door and realised it was an elaborate bell pull. She tried it, and a few moments later a butler appeared.

He was an elderly gentleman with white hair and a thin, ascetic face with a surprising flash of humour in it. 'Yes, ma'am? May I help you?'

She stood on the step shivering. 'I am Clarice Corde, wife of the vicar who is taking Mr Wynter's place this Christmas,' she began.

'Indeed, ma'am. Sir Peter spoke of you. Would you care to come in? It's a distinctly chilly evening.'

'Distinctly,' she agreed through chattering teeth. 'Yes. I need to ask Sir Peter's advice, if I may?'

'Of course.'

The butler stepped back, took her cloak and shawl, and conducted her into the withdrawing room, which was panelled in oak with a coffered ceiling. A magnificent arras hung on the wall, and the fire burning in the hearth was big enough to have roasted a pig on a spit above the flames.

Sir Peter was sitting in a huge, leather armchair by the blaze and he stood up the moment she came in.

The butler offered Clarice tea, which she accepted. She took the seat opposite Sir Peter.

'What may I do to help?' he asked her.

She told him of finding the Bible, and then the address which she knew could not be correct. 'I wonder if you know where he has really gone,' she finished. 'I think he will miss his own scriptures and I would like to send them to him.'

'Indeed,' he said, frowning now. 'How odd that he should forget to pack such a thing. No doubt it was an oversight. He will be searching for it already. But I am afraid I don't know where he has gone. In fact I did not even known he was going. It was a surprise to me. I would have wished him a good journey.

I am sorry I didn't.' There was gentleness in his voice and a softness of genuine regret in his eyes.

Looking at him, Clarice was suddenly aware of how deeply fond of Mr Wynter he must have been, and that perhaps he was more hurt by the rift between them than he admitted.

'You have no idea where else he goes?' she pressed. 'I could at least write a letter and if he writes back, I shall know where to send the Bible. I must not risk losing it.'

'No!' He leaned forward. 'You must keep it safely. Please, don't risk it unless you are absolutely certain where he is. Family Bibles matter intensely . . . so many memories. Could you not be mistaken about this hotel?'

'No.' She had no doubt about it. She had been sorry and inconvenienced to find it changed herself. She told him of her experience. She did not mention that it had been the vicar's personal Bible she had found, not a family one.

A shadow flickered across his face with its delicate lines.

'I see. No, there seems to be no room for error. I'm sorry; I really don't know where else he might have gone. I wish I could offer help.'

The branch of the tree burning in the grate settled a little, and a shower of sparks flew up the vast chimney. Clarice looked around the age and beauty of the room and wondered how many generations of Connaughts had sat here, hearing the stories of the village, helping, protecting, disciplining, governing, and probably using and taxing as well. Walls like these had seen England's history unfolding since before the Spanish Armada had sailed in the time of Queen Elizabeth. Perhaps even Henry VIII had visited here with one of his six wives. Or Walsingham had sent out his spies from here. There might be a priest-hole behind that fireplace for fugitive Catholics in the years they were hunted and burned. Which side had the Connaughts been on in the Civil War? Or the Bloodless Revolution of 1688? She could go on to the present time.

Sir Peter was smiling at her, his eyes bright again in the firelight. 'Would you like to see the house?' he asked. 'It would be my pleasure to show you.'

'I'd love to,' she said sincerely.

He guided her through it all with a kind of gentle pride she found endearing. He did not boast except once, and then immediately apologised for it as though it had been a breach of good manners.

'You have a right to be proud,' she said honestly. 'It is so beautiful, and obviously it has been loved over the centuries. Thank you for your generosity in showing me.'

He looked pleased, even a little self-conscious. 'Are you sure you wish to walk home alone? It is now quite dark.'

'Oh, certainly,' she said with confidence. 'It is only a mile or so.'

'Still, I would rather accompany you, at least as far as the village green. I would be happier.'

She did not argue. When she was within sight of the vicarage lights, which were already familiar to her, he bade her good night and turned back towards the manor. Clarice went another few yards, then saw the dark outline of a figure coming towards her, leaning into the wind and huddling a shawl around her. It was so small and walked with such tiny, hurried steps it had to be a woman.

'Good evening,' Clarice said clearly, thinking the woman had not seen her and was in danger of bumping into her unless she moved off the path into the snow.

'Oh! My dear, you gave me a fright!' the woman exclaimed. 'I was quite lost in my own thoughts. Since I don't know you, you must be the new vicar's wife.'

'Yes. I am. Clarice Corde.' Clarice held out her hand.

'How do you do?' the woman responded. Her voice was husky and a little cracked, but it must have been rich in her youth. 'My name is Sybil Towers,' she went on. 'Welcome to Cottisham. I am sure you will be happy here. We all love Mr Wynter, and we will make you comfortable too.'

'Mrs Towers,' Clarice said impulsively, 'you don't know where Mr Wynter went for his holiday, do you? I have found something he left behind, and I would very much like to send it after him, but the only address I have is not for this year.'

'No! I'm afraid I have no idea,' Mrs Towers responded. 'In fact I didn't even know he was going away. I'm so sorry.'

It would be inexcusable to keep the old lady standing outside in the rising wind any longer, so Clarice dismissed it, wished her good night, and hurried on to the vicarage.

Dominic was at home and intensely relieved to see her, in fact so much so that she found no suitable opportunity to tell him about the Bible, or the fact that she could find no one who knew the vicar's holiday address.

The morning was milder, and thick wet snow blanketed everything. Even the air swirled in white flurries, blocking out the village green so that the houses at the further side were all but invisible. It was a world of movement and shadows seen through a haze.

Dominic left to visit the sick and the lonely, and Clarice began the necessary duties of housework. There was no point in thinking of doing laundry, beyond shirts and underclothing. Nothing else would dry.

She should air the vicar's bedroom. Closed rooms, especially in this weather, could come to smell stale. She did not wish him to return to that stuffy, unoccupied feeling. The cat pattered around behind her, poking its nose into everything and giving her the uncomfortable suspicion that there could be mice here after all. Harry had gone back to sleep in front of the range in the kitchen, as if he were still sulking. He had been outside first thing with Dominic, but now he refused to wag his tail or in any other way respond.

The first thing she noticed in the bedroom – after opening the windows briefly, just to let the cold, sweet air circulate – was a stark drawing of bare trees in the snow. There was no colour in it at all and yet there was a grace to the lines that held her attention. She stared at it so long she was cold when she realised the window was still open. She shut it quickly, and then returned to the picture. It was another of the vicar's own drawings. She had begun to recognise his style even before she read his signature in the corner.

She was glad the vicarage had been designed for a family, and was large enough that they had not needed to use this room. It belonged to Mr Wynter and he should not have to move his belongings to make way for Dominic and her. She looked around it with pleasure, amazed that she could feel such a liking for a man she had never met. People spoke so well of him, he was obviously a man of great compassion. But that might not be personal so much as part of his calling. It was the delicacy, the simple grace of his drawings that showed his nature. He saw extraordinary beauty in a bare branch, the tiny twigs against the light, the strength of a trunk stripped of its summer glory, powerful in its nakedness.

She gazed around the walls at the other pictures. Each was different, and yet all had the same inner qualities. She wondered if he were busy now creating more. Was he out walking in the snow somewhere in East Anglia, selecting just the right scene under the wide, Norfolk skies? Perhaps he would draw the bare coastline and the sea grasses, the wind-riven skies, clouds dragged out in long streamers above the line of the waves.

Reluctantly she made certain the windows were fastened securely and then went back downstairs.

She was tidying the study when she came across a carefully sharpened soft-leaded pencil sitting on top of the chest of narrow drawers near the window. Her first thought was that Dominic had unintentionally sharpened one of the vicar's pencils, before realising what it was.

She should put it away. Perhaps it belonged in one of the drawers. She opened the top one to see, and found a dozen more pencils there, all sharpened. There were also charcoals of various thickness, white pencils, erasers, and a sharp blade – in fact all one needed for drawing. Were they extras?

She closed the drawer and opened the one below. It was full of unused blocks of artist's watercolour paper. He must have a great deal if he had this much to leave behind! Without thinking she pulled open the cupboard door. With a sudden chill she saw the easel, neatly folded. How could he not have taken it with him? This, and his pencils, were the tools of his art!

Mystified, she went back up to his bedroom and shamelessly opened the wardrobe door. There were only four pairs of boots inside: smart black boots for Sundays; a pair of brown boots; a second pair of black boots, definitely older; and stout walking boots for country wear, up to the ankles, thick-soled such as one would choose on a day like this.

There were winter clothes hanging on the rail as well, including an extremely nice woollen overcoat – not city wear, more casual – with a collar to turn up against the worst weather. It was just the sort of coat a man would like for walking in the country or by the sea.

Why had he not taken it with him? And the boots? And for that matter, the stout walking stick leaning against the wall in the corner? To forget the Bible might be an oversight, even the

pencils, or paper, but not the winter clothes as well! There was
something wrong. He had left in haste, and not for pleasure as
Dominic had been told. Was it some family emergency, or
bereavement? Would he be gone until the situation, whatever it
was, had been resolved? Had he a brother or sister in some kind
of trouble? Possibly it was a sudden and serious illness?

When Dominic returned home late, and cold to the bone, she
started to tell him, then realised he was not listening to her. He
heard her words, but not their meaning. He was too deep in his
own fear that he could not find something new and powerful
to say to the people of this village for him to hear the anxiety
within her. And it would be Sunday in two days, and his first
sermon here.

'They are good people,' he said, standing in the sitting room
with his back to the fire, which burned up brightly, thawing out
the cold that chilled and numbed his flesh. 'They know their
scriptures at least as well as I do. The vicar has preached to
them with passion and eloquence, not only at Christmas but all
through the year.' There was a shadow in his eyes, a tightness
across his cheeks. 'What can I say to them that will be anything
more than an echo of what he has already said?' he asked her.
'Any one of them could stand up in the pulpit and tell the
Christmas story as well as I can. Clarice, what can I say to make
it new?'

She saw the spark of fear in his eyes, the knowledge that he
might not be equal to the task that mattered to him so much.
This village was old, comfortable and secure in its habits. It

was not conscious of any hunger that needed filling, any ignorance or darkness waiting for light. They wanted to stay as they were and be reassured that all was well. Anyone could do that; pass and leave no mark at all, like wind over water.

She ached to be able to help him. She was seeing for the first time the need in him: not desire to do a job or fulfil a duty, but a hunger to succeed that would not let him rest or leave him free from pain if he failed.

'What's the best thing about Christmas?' she asked, trying to strip away the trite, all the things that had already been said. 'What does it really mean to us? What . . . what is it for? It's not goodwill, a brief time of peace or generosity. It has to be more than that.'

'It's the beginning of our faith,' he replied. 'Christ coming into the world.' He said it as if it were obvious.

'I know that.' She felt crushed. She was failing him. 'But what for?' she insisted. 'Why is everything different afterwards?'

The fire was scorching him and he stepped away from it. 'I'm not exactly sure how to answer that,' he replied. 'It sounds . . . it sounds too much like an academic answer, and that's not what they need, Clarice. I need a spiritual answer, a joy in the soul.'

She could think of nothing better to add, and feeling empty she turned and went into the kitchen.

Clarice woke to find a white world, silent, deep in snow. The air was motionless and when she opened the back door into the garden to let Harry out, the bitter cold of it was sharp in her lungs and she drew in her breath in amazement at the beauty of it. The old apple tree was laden with snow like an extravagant blossom. Other trees, soaring upwards, were naked, too thin to hold the snow, shining against an enamel sky.

But it was a dangerous beauty, a cold that paralysed, a depth of snow that soaked heavy skirts and exhausted old or fragile limbs. The low, winter sun was almost blinding.

She closed the door and turned to find Dominic standing behind her, a rueful smile on his face.

'You're going out,' she said, more as a statement than a question. She wished he did not have to, but if he had found excuses to stay at home she would have been even more deeply hurt. What use was preaching or praying if you were not willing to act?

'I'll try not to be long,' he answered. 'But there'll be people who shouldn't go out in this, even to fetch wood, never mind to get bread or milk.'

'I know.' She gave him a quick kiss, hugging him tightly for a moment, then going back to the kitchen to tidy up. It was warm in there and she had hot water, which made her more fortunate than many.

However, in the middle of the morning she found with surprise that the coal bucket beside the stove was empty, and the coke scuttle as well. She would have to go down to the cellar to fetch more. What was left would not last until Dominic returned.

She picked up the scuttle and went to the hall. The cellar door was locked, but she had the key on the big household ring and it opened with ease. A rush of chill air engulfed her immediately, making her shiver and step back. There was a swish past her ankles, and Etta disappeared down the steps into the darkness.

'Mice!' Clarice said in disgust. 'I suppose it's your job, but you really are a nuisance. Well, I'm not taking a candle down there. It'll blow out and then I'll not even find my way back.' She put down the coke scuttle and went to look for a lantern. She knew there was one in the scullery by the back door. She found it, lit it, settled the glass to protect the flame, and then returned. Etta was nowhere to be seen.

It was no more than a ten-minute job to fill the coke scuttle, take it back up to the kitchen, and then fill the coal bucket for the sitting-room fire as well.

'Etta!' she called encouragingly. 'Come on, Etta! There's a nice warm fire for you up here, and I'll give you some fresh milk! Better than mice.'

There was no sound, except Harry's feet on the hall floor. He came padding through, looking interested at last, his head on one side, eyebrows cocked.

'She's gone down there after mice,' Clarice explained, then thought how absurd she was being, talking to the animal as if he understood. Actually, she was ridiculously pleased that at last he was taking more notice of her. He went to the door, slithered through the opening and disappeared down the steps. 'Fetch her back up,' Clarice called after him. 'I'm not leaving this door open all morning, it's far too cold.'

She stood hopefully for several minutes, and neither of them reappeared.

'Drat!' she said fiercely. She was now thoroughly chilled and rapidly losing patience, but she really did not feel as if she could close them in. This was their home; she was the interloper. Impatiently she picked up the lantern and went down the steps again.

Neither Harry nor Etta was visible. She held the light higher and up near the far corner, which was where she found the rather narrow entrance to the second cellar. They must be in there. More mice, no doubt. She had not known dogs ate mice too, or perhaps he was just curious.

She went through, her skirts brushing against the sides of the doorway. Now they would be covered in coal dust. Perhaps it would brush off without staining, but then it would still need sweeping up. 'Harry!' she said sharply. 'Etta!' She held the lantern forward and saw them immediately, standing side-by-side, Etta's tail up and bristling, Harry's tail down unhappily. He let out a long, low wail.

Then she saw the crumpled heap beyond them, dark but quite definitely not coal. Her stomach clenched, her hand shaking so the light danced unevenly. She moved forward until it was all horribly clear. An elderly man lay face up on the rubble remains of an old coal heap. His eyes were closed, his gaunt features smeared with dust and dark with what might have been bruises.

A gash was scored across his nose, but any blood had long since dried and darkened.

Clarice breathed in shakily, gasping. The heat drained out of her body as if sucked away. The cat and dog were so close they seemed to be touching each other, as though for comfort. She did not need to question if that were their master; the dog's low howl of grief again was answer enough. Anyway, who else could it be? Even smeared with coal dust she could see bits of the white of his clerical collar.

There was no question if there was anything she could do for him; it was perfectly obvious there was not. Slowly, her knees wobbling, the lantern swaying, she fumbled her way back up the steps again and then stood gulping air at the top. She grasped the door lintel in the grey daylight. She must report the death. The poor old man had probably had a heart attack, or something of the sort. Everyone thought he had gone away, so no one would have missed him and gone to look. What a bitterly sad way for a vicar, of all people, to die. From everyone's account, he had been a fine man, and deeply and justly loved.

She could wait for Dominic to return, but in this weather he could be a long time doing all that was necessary. She did not want to stay here alone, knowing what was downstairs. She was perfectly capable of putting on boots and a cape and going to find the doctor herself. She knew where he lived; that was one of the things Mrs Wellbeloved had told her. It was a stiff walk, but along open road all the way. She would make it in half an hour, even in the snow, and he might have a pony and trap for the way back.

She extinguished the lantern, left the cellar door wedged open, so Harry and Etta could come out if they chose, or stay and mourn if that was their nature. Perhaps that was more fitting anyway. She rather hoped they would. Then she put on the boots, wrapped herself around in her cloak and set out, her mind so filled with pity she scarcely noticed either the cold or the way the deep snow dragged at her feet.

'Heart attack, poor man,' Dr Fitzpatrick told her, coming back up the steps and closing the cellar door behind him. The cat and dog had come upstairs again, persuaded with some difficulty, and were now sitting side by side in front of the kitchen stove. 'Only comfort is he probably felt very little,' Fitzpatrick went on. He was a fussy man with a large moustache. 'Are you all right, Mrs Corde? Horrible experience for you. What on earth were you doing down there?'

She had already explained to him, or she thought she had. Perhaps she had been more incoherent than she supposed. 'I went to fill the coke scuttle, and the cat came too, and then I couldn't find her.'

He nodded. 'Smelled something, I suppose. Or perhaps just after the mice.' He held up his coal-smeared hands.

'Oh, I'm sorry,' Clarice apologised quickly. 'Please come into the kitchen and wash, and perhaps you'd like a cup of tea?' She glanced down at his sodden trouser legs where the snow on them had melted in the warmth of the house, then her own heavy, wet skirts.

'Yes,' he accepted with alacrity. 'Thank you.'

She busied herself with water in the kettle, warming the teapot, fetching milk from a very chilly pantry, and offering him a slice of cake, which he made an excuse for accepting as well.

'I'll take care of the arrangements,' he said with his mouth full. 'I dare say they won't be able to hold a funeral for a few days, considering the weather, and what the bishop might care to do, but I'll have the body removed and all the appropriate registrations dealt with. You don't need to concern yourself, Mrs Corde. I will take care of it all. And I would be obliged if you would speak of this to no one yet. There is a proper order of things, which we must observe.'

'Thank you.' She felt relieved, but more than a little sad. It was a lonely and undignified way to go. Not that she supposed Mr Wynter had been more than briefly aware of it. He had lived well, very well, and in the end that was all that mattered. 'Thank you,' she repeated. 'No doubt my husband will be in touch with the bishop. He may . . . he may wish us to remain a little longer.' She realised as she said the words how much she hoped that he would – a lot longer, perhaps always.

It was ten minutes later, with the doctor on his second cup of tea, when Dominic came in, slamming the front door behind him and striding down the hall, shedding snow everywhere.

'Clarice!' he called urgently, fear edging his voice sharply. 'Clarice!'

She came to the door immediately, and almost ran into him. His coat was wet, his face whipped red by the cold, his eyes frightened. As soon as he saw her he was flooded with relief. 'Someone told me you sent for the doctor urgently. What is it? Were they wrong?'

She could not help smiling. It was wonderful, and still faintly surprising to her, that he should care so intensely. 'I'm perfectly well,' she said, almost all the shiver gone out of her voice. 'I went for coke in the cellar and the cat got into another cellar beyond. I found the vicar's body. The poor man had, it seems, gone down there and had a heart attack. I felt the doctor was the best person to inform.' She met his eyes, looking to see if he understood what she had done.

He was momentarily shocked. 'Dead? Mr Wynter? You mean he has been down there all the time?'

'Yes. Don't look like that,' she added gently. She touched his hand. 'There was nothing we could have done for him.'

The doctor drank the last of his tea and came into the hall.

'Fitzpatrick,' he introduced himself. 'You must be Mr Corde. Sad thing to happen. So sorry your poor wife had to be the one to find him.' He shook his head. 'But I'll take care of all the details. Perhaps you'd just give me a hand to carry the poor old man up the steps, then I can fetch the blacksmith's cart and have him taken away. My trap is rather too small, you know.'

'Yes, of course,' Dominic agreed quickly, beginning to take off his heavy outdoor coat.

It was an awkward job up the cellar stairs, and required both men, so Clarice walked ahead of them with the lantern. On the way back up again she moved ahead and laid a clean blanket on the kitchen table so they could put him down gently on it. As soon as it was accomplished, the doctor went to find the blacksmith.

'I think I should clean him up a bit,' Clarice said very quietly. Her throat ached and she found it hard to swallow.

Dominic offered to do it, but she insisted. Laying out the dead was a job for women. She would wash the coal dust from his head and face and hands. She did it with hot, soapy water, very gently, as if he could still feel pain. He had had fine features, aquiline and sensitive, but they were hollow now, in death. There was a bad scrape on his nose, as if he had struck it falling – and yet they had found him on his back, and to re-inforce that fact, there was a deep gash in the back of his head. He must have gone down hard.

In straightening his legs, Clarice also noticed that his trousers were slightly torn at the shins, and the skin underneath abraded and bruised.

'How did he do that?' she said curiously.

'It happened before he died,' Dominic said quietly. 'People don't bruise after the heart stops. He must have stumbled as he went down the steps. Perhaps he wasn't feeling very well even then.'

'I wonder why he went down at all,' she said thoughtfully, pulling the fabric straight. 'The buckets of coal and coke were all full.'

'I expect Mrs Wellbeloved filled them,' he pointed out.

She looked at him almost apologetically. 'If she'd gone down there, and he had the buckets with him, then why didn't she find him?'

'What are you suggesting, Clarice?'

'I don't know,' she admitted. 'I just wondered why he went down there, and nobody knew.'

'They thought he had gone away on holiday,' he answered. 'We all did.'

She frowned. 'Why? Why did the bishop think he was going on holiday?'

'Because he wrote and told him,' Dominic said.

She said nothing. Something made her more than sad, but she was not sure what it was.

There was a voice at the door, calling out urgently. Dominic turned and went back to the hall. 'What is it? Can I help?'

'Oh, Vicar!' It was a man's voice, deep and unfamiliar. 'Poor Mrs Hapgood's had bad news, and she's that upset, I don't know what to do for her. Can you come? Dreadful state, she's in, poor thing.'

Dominic hesitated, turning back towards Clarice.

She knew how much it mattered; this was their chance to prove they could do everything that a parish needed. 'Yes, of course you can,' she said firmly. There was no need to tell this man that Mr Wynter was dead. He had his own griefs to aid first. 'There's nothing here I can't take care of.'

'Oh, bless you, ma'am!' the man in the hall said fervently. 'This way, Vicar.'

The doctor came back with the blacksmith and his cart, and the two men carried the body out quickly and discreetly, wrapped in a blanket. After they had gone Clarice went back to the kitchen and washed the few dishes they had used, her mind whirling. There was something wrong. She could not put her finger on it, standing here at the bench. She would have to go down to the cellar again, and yet she was reluctant to. It was more than the cold, or even the memory of what she had found.

'Come on, Harry,' she said briskly. 'Come, keep me company.' She relit the lantern and the dog, surprisingly, obeyed her. It was the very first time he had done as she told him. Together they went to the door and opened it. She went first down the steps, very carefully, and he followed behind. A little more than halfway he stopped and sniffed.

'What is it?' she said, gulping, her hand swaying so the light gyrated around the walls.

Harry sniffed again and looked up at her.

Swallowing hard she retraced her steps back up to him and bent to examine it. It was a very small piece of fabric, no more than a few threads caught in a splinter of the wood. At first she thought how odd it was that the dog had noticed it, then she saw the smear of blood also. It was not much darker than the coal-smudged steps themselves; only when she licked her finger and touched it, it came away red. Was this where the vicar had fallen, and then gone on down the rest of the way to the floor? How could she find out?

She held the lantern so she could see the steps closely. They were dark with years of trodden-in coal dust, each bit dropped from a bucket or scuttle carried up full. No matter how closely she looked, all she could distinguish were the most recent marks: a heel dent, and the smear of a sole. They could have been anybody's: Dominic's, the doctor's, even Mrs Wellbeloved's.

She went to the bottom and looked again, not expecting to find anything, or knowing what it would mean even if she did.

Then she saw it: a small, neat pattern of marks she understood very easily – cat prints. Etta had been this way. She walked after the marks, for no real reason except that they led to the second cellar, and they were easy to read because they were on plain ground, as if someone had swept all the old marks away with a broom. Why would anybody sweep just a single track, no more than eighteen or twenty inches wide? It was not even clean, just brushed once. Several times it was disturbed at the sides by footprints.

Then she understood. It was not swept – they were drag marks. Someone had pulled something heavy, covered in cloth, from the bottom of the stairs over into the second cellar.

Could Mr Wynter have fallen, struck his head and become confused, mistaken where he was and dragged himself in the wrong direction?

No. That was idiotic. There were no handprints in the dust. And his hands would have been filthy when they found him. They weren't: only smudges here and there – the backs as much as the palms.

She was in the second cellar now. When she had found him

he had been lying on his back. But his nose had been scraped, as if he had fallen forward. And there was coal dust on his front as well as his back. The hard, deep wound was on the back of his head.

'Somebody killed him, Harry,' she said softly, putting her hand out to touch the dog's soft fur. 'Somebody hit him on the head and dragged him in here, and then left him. Why would they do that? He was an old man whom almost everyone loved. What did he know that was so terrible?'

The dog whined and leaned his weight against her leg.

'I don't suppose you know, and even if you did, you can't tell me.' She was talking to him because it was a lot better not to be alone. 'So I'll have to find out without you. *We'll* have to,' she corrected. 'I'll tell Dominic when he comes back. Right now, in case anybody calls, I think we should pretend that we don't know anything at all. Come on. It's cold down here, and we shouldn't stay anyway. It isn't safe.'

When Dominic returned from his visits, tired and cold, she had no alternative but to tell him immediately. It was already mid-afternoon and there would be little more than an hour before the light began to fade, and the ground froze even harder.

'What?' he said incredulously, sitting at the kitchen table, his hands thawing as he held the cup of tea she had made. 'Are you sure?'

'Yes, I am sure,' she said, looking at him steadily. 'I'm not being overimaginative, Dominic. Remember the marks on his face and head? Remember how little coal dust there was on his hands? Or on his knees? But there was a tear on the shin of his trousers, and dust where he had been dragged. Go down to the cellar and look. It's still there.'

He hesitated.

'Please,' she urged. 'I don't want to be the only one who saw it. Anyway, I don't think the doctor is going to listen to me.'

She was perfectly correct – Dr Fitzpatrick did not believe either of them.

'That suggestion is preposterous,' he said irritably, pulling on his moustache. 'It is a perfectly ordinary domestic tragedy. An elderly man had a heart attack and fell down the cellar stairs. Or perhaps he simply tripped and then the shock of the fall brought on an attack. He was confused, naturally; perhaps hurt, and he mistakenly crawled in the wrong direction. You are trying to make a horror out of something which is merely sad. And if I may say so, that is a completely irresponsible thing to do.'

Clarice took a deep breath, facing his anger. 'What did he go into the cellar for?' she asked.

'My dear Mrs Corde, surely that is perfectly obvious?' Fitzpatrick snapped. 'Exactly the same reason as you did yourself! For coal!'

She met his gaze steadily. 'I took a lantern and a coal bucket, and I left the door open at the top,' she replied.

'Then perhaps he went for some other reason,' Fitzpatrick said. 'Didn't you say something about the dog? He must have gone to look for it.'

'Why would you go to look for anything in a cellar without a lantern?' Dominic pressed him. 'It doesn't make sense.'

'He probably stood at the top and called.' Fitzpatrick was becoming more and more annoyed. His face was tight, lips thin. 'Reverend, you are a guest here. In view of poor Wynter's death, it will possibly be for far longer than you had originally intended. You are now required to guide the village through a sad and very trying time. As shepherd of the people, it is your calling to sustain, comfort and uplift them, not indulge in what, I have to say, is idle and vicious speculation on the death of a deeply loved man. I am sorry that it falls to my lot to remind you of this. Don't make it necessary for me to take it further.'

Dominic's face flamed, but he turned and left without retaliation. He could not afford it, as the doctor had reminded him.

Clarice went with him, not daring to meet Fitzpatrick's eyes in case he saw in hers the rage she felt towards him. He had humiliated Dominic, and that she had no idea how to heal, so she could not forgive him for it. As she went out into the snow, she remembered her father telling her that if you sought wealth or fame, other people might dislike you for it, but if you sought only to do good, no one would be your enemy. How wrong he was! Good held a mirror to other people's hearts, and the reflection was too often unflattering. People could hate you for that more than for almost anything else.

She caught up with Dominic and linked her arm through his, holding on to him when he tried to pull back. He was ashamed because he had not found a way to stand up for the truth. She struggled for something to say that would make it better, not worse. If she were to sound trite it would be worse than silence; it would be patronising, as if she thought him not strong enough to face their failure. Yet she ached to comfort him. If she could not at least do that, what use was she?

'I'm sorry,' she said a trifle abruptly. 'I shouldn't have urged you to speak to him so quickly. Perhaps if we had waited until tomorrow, and thought harder, we might have persuaded him.'

'No we wouldn't,' he said grimly. 'He doesn't want to think that anyone would kill Mr Wynter.'

'I don't want to either!' she said hotly. 'I hate thinking it. But I have to follow what my sense tells me. And I don't believe you go into the cellar alone in the dark to fetch coal, to look for a cat or dog, or anything else. If he'd fallen down then Mrs Wellbeloved would have found him. The door would have been open . . .'

'Maybe when she came in the front door the wind slammed the cellar door shut?' he suggested.

'It faces the other way,' she pointed out. 'It would have blown it wider open.'

'Well, what do you think did happen?' he asked. They were walking side by side along the road, their feet making the only tracks in the new snow. In the east the sky was darkening.

'I think someone came in and said or did something to make him go into the cellar, then pushed him,' she answered. 'When he was at the bottom, perhaps crumpled over, stunned, they hit him on the back of the head, hard enough to kill him, whether they meant that or not. Although I can't see why they would do it unless they intended him to die. They could hardly explain it away.' Her mind was racing. The rising wind was edged with ice and she blinked against it. 'Then they dragged him into the other cellar, so he wouldn't be found too soon—'

'Why?' he interrupted. 'What difference would it make?'

'So nobody knows when it happened, of course.' The ideas came to her as she spoke. 'That way nobody could have been proved to be here at the right time. Then they closed the door, and probably took his cases away, so people would think he had already gone on his holiday. Only they forgot about his painting things . . . and his favourite Bible.'

He was frowning. 'Do you really think so? Why? That doesn't sound like a quarrel in the heat of some . . . some dispute. It's perfectly deliberate and cold-blooded.'

'Yes it is,' she agreed reluctantly. 'I suppose he must have known something about one of the people here that was so terrible to them that they couldn't afford to trust that he would never tell anyone.'

'He couldn't tell,' Dominic angered. 'They would know that. Not if it were confessed to him. No priest would.'

'Then maybe it wasn't confessed to him.' She would not let go of the idea. 'Perhaps he found it out some other way. He knew lots of things about all sorts of people. He would have to. He's been here in Cottisham for ages. He must have seen a great deal.'

'What could possibly be worth killing over?' He was putting up a last fight against believing.

'I don't know,' Clarice admitted. 'That's what we have to find out.'

'But he wrote to the bishop saying he was going on holiday,' he pointed out. 'So he obviously intended to. Is that coincidence?'

'Did he?' she asked. 'Or did someone else write, copying his hand? It wouldn't be too difficult, and if the bishop did not look closely, or compare it with other letters, it would be easy enough. And plenty of people in the village could have letters or notes Mr Wynter had written at one time or another.'

Dominic said nothing, trudging steadily through the snow. The light was fading rapidly and the shadows under the trees were already impenetrable.

'We have to find out,' she insisted quietly, her voice heavy with the burden of what she was thinking. She would very much rather have been able to say they should let it go, pretend they had never known, but it would be a lie that would grow sharper all the time, like a blister on the tender skin of your feet. 'Christ was kind, He forgave,' she went on. 'But He never moderated the truth to make people like Him, or pretended that something was all right when it wasn't, because that would be easier. I think Mr Wynter was killed for something he knew. What do you think, really?' She took a deep breath and let it out slowly. 'I'll do whatever you decide.' That was so difficult to say.

He gave an almost jerky little laugh. 'You can't do that, Clarice. You'd grow to hate me. I think he was probably killed. Either way, I can't pretend I don't know. Mr Wynter deserves better; and if someone did kill him, then they deserve better

58

too. They need justice more than he does. Justice heals in the end, if you allow it to.' He walked a few more yards in silence. 'I suppose we need to find out what he knew, and about whom.'

A wave of relief swept over her. 'We'll begin in the village,' she said. 'We can't get out of it now, anyway.'

'Whom do we trust?' he asked, glancing at her quickly.

'No one,' she said simply. 'We can't afford to. We have no idea who it was.'

They spent a long, quiet evening by the fire. Neither of them talked very much, but it was one of the most companionable times she could remember, in spite of the ugly task that awaited them the following day. The flames crackled and the coals grew yellow hot in the heart of it. The snow deepened in blanketing silence outside, except for the occasional whoosh as it grew too heavy on the steep roof and slid off to the ground. There was nothing to discuss – they were in agreement.

On Monday, the wind sliced in from the east like a whetted knife. Straight after breakfast Dominic set out to make his calls.

Sunday had been awful. Dominic was so anxious he barely spoke to her as he ate breakfast before church. He picked up books and put them down again, found quotes, then discarded them. One minute he wanted to be daring, challenge people to new thought, the next to be gentle, to reassure them in all the old beliefs, comfort the wounds of loneliness, and misunderstanding, and say nothing that might awaken troubling ideas or demand any change.

A dozen times Clarice drew in her breath to say that he had

no time, in three short weeks, to stay within safe bounds. No one would listen; certainly no one would remember anything about it afterwards.

She nearly said so, then she saw his slender hand on the back of the chair, and that the knuckles were white. This was not the right time. But she was afraid there never would be the time. The next sermon would be for Christmas. One pedestrian sermon now, safe and colourless, might be all it would take to lose their sympathy, and their hope.

'Don't quote,' she said suddenly. 'Don't use other people's words. Whatever they are, they'll have heard them before.'

'People like repetition,' he said with a bleak smile, his eyes dark with anxiety and the crushing weight of doubt Spindlewood had laid on him.

In that moment Clarice hated Spindlewood for what he had done with his mealy mouth and grudging, time-serving spirit. 'Tell them what you said to me about courage, and how it's the one virtue without which all others may be lost,' she urged him. 'You meant it! Tell them.'

He did, passionately, eloquently, without repeating himself. She had no idea whether they were impressed or not. They spoke politely to him afterwards, even with warmth, but there was no ease among them. Everyone was in their Sunday best, and they walked home through the snow in silence.

Clarice started where she had traditionally been told lay the root of all evil, although actually she thought it was far more likely to find its roots in selfishness – and perhaps self-right-eousness, which was not such a different thing, when you thought about it. Still, money was easier to measure, and the vicar's ledgers were readily available, both from the church and from the household.

She had barely begun examining when she was interrupted by the arrival of Mrs Wellbeloved, carrying two hard, white cabbages and a string of very large onions. She looked extremely pleased with herself, stamping her feet and shedding snow everywhere.

'Said as it would be cold. Tree fell over with the weight of it and the road south's blocked.' She announced it as a personal victory. ''Less you want to go all round Hertford an' the like. An' there's no saying you can get through that either. Could all be closed.'

'Then we are very fortunate to have coal and food,' Clarice replied warmly.

'Onions.' Mrs Wellbeloved put them on the table. Not that anyone could have mistaken them for something else.

'Thank you.' Clarice smiled at her. She already knew from the brief glance she had had at the accounts that Mrs Wellbeloved had done all the shopping for the vicar. Clarice wanted to tell her of their discovery of the body in the cellar, but Fitzpatrick had asked them not to, and his implication had been clear enough. Still Clarice felt guilty saying nothing. 'That's very kind of you,' she added.

Mrs Wellbeloved smiled, her face pink. She began to take off her overcoat and prepare to scrub the floor.

It was half-past eleven before Clarice could return to the ledger and read it carefully. She had gone through it twice before she noticed the tiny anomalies. They were sometimes of a shilling or two, but more often just pennies. The mistakes seemed to be in Reverend Wynter's own money, which he accounted very carefully, as anyone on a church stipend had to. Clarice herself knew where every farthing went. The expression 'poor as a church mouse' was not an idle one.

The church accounts, including the donations signed for by John Boscombe until a few months ago, and more recently by William Frazer, were accurate, then inaccurate, then accurate again. The final sum was always as it should be.

Clarice could understand how people ended up chewing pencils. It made no sense. Why on earth would anyone steal tuppence, or even less? She was convinced it was not carelessness, because the same figures kept recurring in what she realised was a sequence. She placed them side by side, according to date, and then she saw the pattern. The few pence went missing from the church accounts, then from Mr Wynter's personal account. Finally the church accounts were correct again. Someone was taking tiny amounts from the collection for the poor box, irregular and always very small. Mr Wynter was replacing them from his own money.

But why? Would it not have been the right thing to do to find out who was the thief – if that was not too serious a word for such petty amounts? Might it be a child? Perhaps he did not want to have such an accusation made when it would become uglier than a simple question of family discipline.

Who could she ask? Perhaps William Frazer would know, or have an idea? He lived next to the village store, and even in this weather she could walk there quite easily. Of course she would not go across the green. One could barely see where the pond was, never mind avoid treading on the ice beneath the snow, and perhaps falling in.

But Frazer had no idea. 'I'm so sorry, Mrs Corde,' he said earnestly as she sat in the small, crowded room by his parlour fire, still shivering from her journey in the snow. The wind seemed to find its way through even the thickest cloak, and a hat was useless to protect the neck or ears. Now she was almost singeing at the front, and her back was still cold from the draft behind her.

'Your records are immaculate,' she said as flatteringly as she could. 'At the end of the day the money is always correct, but somewhere along the way a few pennies disappear, and then turn up again. It looks as if Mr Wynter made up the difference himself.'

He looked startled, his round face pale with anxiety. 'Why on earth would he do such a thing?' he demanded. 'John Boscombe never said anything to me, and he's as honest as the day. Ask anyone. If there'd been any irregularities, he'd have told me.'

'Perhaps if Mr Wynter knew who it was, he might have asked Mr Boscombe not to say anything,' she suggested, puzzled herself.

'Why would he do that?' Frazer's voice was sharp. 'More like the old gentleman lost a few pence here and there.' He nodded. 'Can happen to anyone. Got the wrong change by mistake, p'raps. Or dropped it in the street and couldn't find it. Done that myself. Only pennies, you said?'

'Yes.'

'Don't worry about it. Dare say you'll keep better books yourself, being younger and seeing a good bit clearer. Should have had spectacles, maybe.'

'Perhaps.' But she did not agree. She thanked him and went out into the bitter wind to walk all the way to John Boscombe's house. He too was at home, kept from his work in the fields by the smothering snow.

'Come in, come in!' he said warmly as he almost pulled her into the hallway and slammed the door against the wind behind her. 'What a day! It's going to be a hard Christmas if it goes on like this. You must be frozen. Let's dust the snow off you before it thaws and gets you wet.' He suited the action to the word without waiting for her to agree, sending snow flying all over the hallway. Fortunately the floor was polished stone, so it would mop up well enough. 'Come into the kitchen,' he invited her, satisfied with his work and turning to lead the way. 'Have some soup. Always keep a stockpot on the simmer this time of the year. The children are out playing. They've built a snowman bigger than I am. Genny! New vicar's wife is here!'

Genevieve Boscombe stood in the middle of the kitchen with

her hands in a big bowl of flour and pastry. She was smiling, but she did not make any move to stop what she was doing.

'Welcome,' she said cheerfully. 'I'll not shake your hand, or I'll have you covered. John'll get you a dish of soup. It's just barley and bones, but it's hot.' There was a faint flush of defiance in her cheeks, from more than just the exertion of rolling the pastry.

One was not defensive unless one was vulnerable. Clarice knew that from her own experience. She was conscious of her clumsiness, where her sisters and her mother had been graceful. The comparison, even made in what was intended as humour, had sometimes hurt her sharply. Once or twice when she had fancied herself in love, she had felt it even more.

She smiled at Mrs Boscombe, deliberately avoiding looking around the kitchen, though she had noticed the good linen sheets that were over the airing rail had been carefully cut down the worn-out middle, and turned to be joined at the sides – to give them longer life. The china on the dresser was good, but a few pieces were chipped, one or two even broken and glued very carefully together. They had had money and were now making do and mending. Even Genevieve's dress indicated the same thing. It was of good quality, but had been up-to-date two years ago.

'Thank you. I would like that very much.' She thought of adding something about barley being very light and pleasing, and decided not to; it would so easily sound patronising. 'Actually I called because I hoped Mr Boscombe might be able to help me with a little of the church bookkeeping,' she said hastily. 'I do so much wish to be accurate. I tried Mr Frazer, but he was unable to offer any assistance.'

'What is the difficulty, Mrs Corde?' Boscombe said with concern.

Genevieve served the barley soup into a blue and white bowl and set it on the table in front of Clarice, who thanked her. Suddenly she realised how difficult it was to explain her problem without lying, at least by implication.

Boscombe was waiting, eyes wide.

She must speak. 'I . . . I was going through Mr Wynter's account books and I found certain . . .'

He was staring at her, something in his look darkening.

She could think of nothing to excuse what she had done, except the truth. Fitzpatrick had no authority to order her silence. Everyone would have to know at some time, perhaps even by tomorrow. She plunged in.

'Mr Wynter is dead,' she said very quietly, sadness overwhelming her. 'We found his body quite by chance . . . in the second cellar. I went for coal and the cat followed me down. I . . .' She looked at him and saw the shock in his face, followed immediately by a terrible regret. He turned to look at Genevieve, who had stopped work and was now listening, then back at Clarice.

'I'm so sorry,' he said a little huskily. 'What happened? I . . . I hadn't heard.'

'No one has,' she said quietly. 'Dr Fitzpatrick asked us not to tell anyone until the bishop has been informed, but . . .' This was the difficult part. 'But we disagree upon what happened. However, I would be grateful if you would not let people know that I told you, at least not yet.'

'Of course not,' he agreed. 'That is why you were going through the account books?' He still seemed puzzled, but there was an inexplicable sense of relief in him, almost as if this were not what he had feared.

'Yes.' She knew she had not yet said enough for him to under-stand. It was unavoidable now. 'You see . . .' What she had planned sounded ridiculous.

'Yes?'

Clarice felt the heat burn up her face. 'You see, I don't believe he died by accident,' she said. She hated the sound of her voice. It was wobbly and absurd. She cleared her throat. 'I think someone hit him. He had injuries both on his face and on the back of his head. They may not have meant to kill him, but . . .' she was telling them too much, '. . . but there was someone else there, and they didn't tell anyone.' She turned from Boscombe to Genevieve. 'He was lying all by himself in the second cellar, but he had no lantern,' she went on. 'Who'd go into a cellar without a lantern?'

'No one,' Genevieve said quietly. 'But why would anyone quarrel with Mr Wynter? He was the nicest man . . .' She stopped.

For a moment they all three were silent: Clarice and Boscombe at the kitchen table, Genevieve standing with the bowl still in her arms.

'Do you think it's the money in the church accounts?' Boscombe asked finally, his face smooth, his eyes avoiding Genevieve's. 'Surely there's hardly enough there to provoke a quarrel?'

'No,' Clarice agreed. 'It's only pennies missing, a shilling or two at the most. But it happened a lot of times, over six months or more.'

Genevieve was looking at Boscombe, staring at him.

Boscombe sat still, his back stiff.

He knows, Clarice thought, the conviction growing in her mind. He knows Mr Wynter was putting the money back. But had he known who was taking it? Was that what he has been trying to find out all those months, and had at last succeeded? And was killed for? No, that was absurd. As she had said before, it was pennies!

Boscombe was watching her, his face tense with concentration, waiting.

'You knew, didn't you?' Clarice said very softly. 'Is . . . is that why you stopped working with Mr Wynter? Because you knew he was protecting someone who . . .'

His eyes were wide, his face almost comical with disbelief.

'You didn't . . .' she answered her own question.

'No! Oh, I knew there were pennies missing here and there,' he assured her, shifting a little in his seat. 'At first I thought it was just that Mr Wynter was a bit careless, or even that he wasn't very good at his sums. Then I realised that in the end the figures were always exactly right, so he knew someone was taking bits and pieces. But I didn't object to his dealing with it in his own way.'

'Did he know who it was?' she asked.

Boscombe smiled. 'He didn't tell me.'

She knew he was speaking the literal truth, but there was a real truth, a more whole and honest one, that he was concealing. 'But he knew,' she insisted. 'As you did?'

'No, I didn't. But even if I had, Mrs Corde, I'm not sure that I would be free to tell you.'

She leaned forward a little across the table, her elbows on its pale, scrubbed wood. 'I think Mr Wynter was killed by someone, Mr Boscombe. They may not have set out to, but they hit him, and when he was dead, or dying . . .' she saw him wince, but she went on, '. . . they dragged him into the further cellar and took the lantern to go back upstairs, leaving him alone there in the dark, for days. It may not have anything to do with the money – it's so small it's meaningless – but it has to do with something!'

Genevieve shivered. 'If that's true, John, then an awful thing has happened. Perhaps you should tell Mr Corde, even if you can't tell Mrs Corde.'

He looked at her at last. 'Mr Wynter knew,' he admitted. 'At least I believe he did, but it was something else, something bigger behind it, and he wanted to know what that was. The greater sin.'

'Do you suppose he found out?' Clarice asked him.

He bit his lip. Now his face was pale. They were talking

about something so dark it had caused the death of a good man, and perhaps the damnation of another.

'I prefer to think not,' he said slowly. 'At least for as long as I can think it.'

'But, John . . .' Genevieve began, and then her voice trailed away.

'I don't know,' he said again. 'And that's the truth.'

Clarice could draw no more from him. She thanked them both and left as the children trooped in from the garden, bright-faced, eyes dancing, skin glowing from the exertion. Their voices were louder than they realised in the sudden confines of the warm kitchen with its scrubbed table and floor, its familiar, odd precious china and the smell of drying linen and herbs. Violence seemed like a dirty word – and utterly inappropriate.

It was early afternoon when Dominic decided to call at the manor house. He had to put his trust in someone, or else simply abandon the idea of finding out exactly how Mr Wynter had died. It still seemed an absurd idea that anyone could have killed him.

It was below freezing, even at this hour, and his feet crunched on the snow. He walked as quickly as he could, his mind racing also. The decision he made now could affect the rest of his life, and of more urgent importance to him, Clarice's life also. She had given up much to marry him, and he wanted passionately that she should never regret that. He found to his surprise that he loved her more with each passing month as he learned to know her better. She had an honesty of mind that was brighter, more translucent than any he had imagined. He kept thinking he knew her, and then she said or did something that surprised him. She made him laugh, even when he did not want to. She never complained about the lack of money, the small, grubby accommodations she had to make to poverty, or to Spindlewood's petty officiousness.

Then she would blow up with temper over an injustice, and put into irretrievable words exactly what he had been thinking, only he had been wise enough not to say it. Or was it cowardly enough? Or was he simply older and more acquainted with the infinite possibilities of failure?

He did not want to disappoint her. She was still so much in love with him. He could see it in her eyes, the sudden flush to her skin if she caught him looking at her with his own emotions too naked in his face. Could he ever live up to what she thought of him? Sometimes being handsome was not a blessing. It led people – women – to hope more of you than you could live up to; it ignited dreams that were too big for the reality of what any man could be.

The manor house loomed up ahead, rising out of the virgin snow as the dark trees of the driveway parted. That was a dream in stone. Did Peter Connaught ever feel the weight of past glory crushing him? Did the ghosts expect too much?

Was Clarice building a drama of murder out of a simple domestic tragedy, weaving together facts into a picture that would create sorrow and injustice, not solve it?

Dominic remembered with a shiver his first acquaintance with her family, with her beautiful, selfish and deadly mother, so locked in her own obsession that reality ceased to exist, every fact bent to serve her delusions about Dominic, and love.

Clarice had been the bravest then, the most willing to see and accept the truth, whatever the pain, or the price.

He lengthened his stride. He would believe her this time. Better to have pursued it and been proven wrong, then run away into blind comfort, and turned his back on truth. That would lie between them always.

He reached the great oak front door and pulled the bell. It was beginning to snow again, in huge white flakes like petals.

The door opened and the butler welcomed him in. Sir Peter was in his office, but he came within moments, smiling, offering tea and crumpets, apologising because he thought there was almost certainly no cake.

'We should have mince pies,' he said, shaking his head. 'I'll make sure we have them next time you come.'

'Just tea would be excellent, thank you,' Dominic answered, following Peter's elegant figure into the huge withdrawing room. 'And a little of your time.' The warmth engulfed him like an embrace. The dog in front of the hearth stood up and stretched luxuriously, then padded over to see who he was, and make sure he should be allowed in.

'What can I do for you?' Peter asked when they were seated. 'How are you settling in?'

'I'm afraid I have very hard news indeed,' Dominic replied. 'I have been told not to break it yet, but—'

'You are not leaving?' Peter said in alarm.

'No. Not in the foreseeable future.' Dominic was startled by how passionately he meant that. He longed to stay here, to be his own master, free to succeed – or fail – on his own beliefs, not Spindlewood's.

'I would like not to leave at all, but that is up to the bishop.'

'I don't understand,' Peter said, confusion clear in his dark face.

As briefly as possible, Dominic told him what had happened, including Fitzpatrick's admonition to tell no one yet, and his own reason for not obeying.

'Oh dear,' Peter said quietly. He looked crushed. 'I liked him enormously, you know.'

Dominic believed him; he did not even have to weigh it in his mind. The sorrow in Peter's face was real – a pain one could sense in the room almost like a third presence.

'The more I learn of him, the more I realise how much he was loved,' Dominic said gently. 'I feel a loss myself, and I never even met him. That is why I intend to find out what happened. I don't know whom to trust, or where to begin.' He smiled ruefully, a trifle self-conscious. 'I have a brother-in-law who is a policeman, a detective. Suddenly I appreciate how appallingly difficult his job is. I have no real authority to ask anyone questions. I am an outsider here, no matter how much I want to belong, but I feel a duty to find the truth of how Mr Wynter died.'

Peter frowned. 'Do you not think perhaps it was an accident more than deliberate, and someone panicked, felt guilty for provoking a quarrel, and so denied it, even to themselves?' His voice dropped to little more than a whisper. 'We can be at our ugliest when we are frightened. I have seen men act quite outside what one had believed their character to be.'

'Certainly,' Dominic agreed. 'But there is a cowardice in that, and a certain brutality in allowing him to lie there undiscovered, which speaks of a terrible selfishness. I don't intend to allow that to go unaddressed. It . . . it seems as if I were saying it doesn't matter, and it does.'

'Of course it does.' Peter lifted his eyes and met Dominic's levelly. 'What can I do to help? I have no idea as to who could, or would have done such a thing.'

'Or why?' Dominic asked.

Peter's mouth pinched very slightly. 'Or why,' he conceded. He drew in his breath as if to add something, and then changed his mind and remained silent.

Dominic wondered what he had been going to say. Surely that it must be a secret Mr Wynter had learned, possibly even by accident, but that someone cared about so passionately, with such fear of loss, that they had killed rather than risk it being known. It was the obvious thing, if a priest were murdered. Could Peter have not said it for any reason except that he knew, or feared it was true?

His own secret, or someone else's?

What secret could the elegant, charming and secure Peter

Connaught care about enough to commit murder? Or who was the friend for whom he would condone such an act?

Anything? Anyone? The most ordinary surface could hide stories of pain the outsider would never imagine. He had quarrelled with Wynter himself to the point where, in spite of their very real affection, he had suddenly stopped calling at the vicarage, and Wynter had put away the chess set and apparently never played again.

Dominic considered challenging him, and decided not to, at least not yet. 'I might be able to narrow it to some degree by knowing who called on him after the last time he was seen alive,' he said aloud.

Peter relaxed fractionally. The difference in his posture in the big chair was so slight it was no more than an easing in the tiny wrinkles in the way his jacket lay, but Dominic was aware of it.

A log settled in the fireplace, sending up a shower of sparks. Peter stood up and placed another, then waited a moment to make certain it was balanced. The flames reached higher to embrace it.

'That seems like a good idea,' he said, taking his seat again. 'If I can help, I should be happy to. I might even be able to make some discreet enquiries myself.'

'I should be most grateful,' Dominic accepted. He had no idea how far to trust him, but sometimes one could learn as much from a lie as from the truth. Even omissions could tell you something. 'Thank you,' he said with warmth. 'I hope that, as you say, it may turn out to be no worse than a grubby accident someone failed to report.'

Peter smiled. 'A weakness not easy to forgive, but not impossible.'

Dominic remained another fifteen minutes, and then took his leave out into a fading afternoon, now even more bitterly cold. Some of the cloud had cleared away and the light was pale with the amber of the fading sun low on the horizon. Shadows were growing longer and the edge of the wind cut like a blade, making his skin hurt and his eyes water.

His feet slipped a little on the ice as he trudged down the drive. Other than the thud of the mounded snow on the evergreens overbalancing on to the ground below, there was silence in the gathering gloom.

Beyond the trees the village lights shone yellow, making little golden smudges sparkling against the blue-grey of twilight. Someone opened a door on to a world of brilliance. A dog scampered out, and then back in again, and the light vanished.

Dominic's hands and feet were numb. He was hunching his shoulders. His ears ached, and also the bones of his face. He stopped for a moment to retie his scarf.

That was when he heard the footsteps behind him. He swung around, his breath catching in his throat, powerful with its knife-edge into the lungs. The figure was there, crossing the village green only a few yards away. She was bent, shivering, and very small. She stopped also, motionless, as if uncertain whether to try running away.

But who could run in the deep snow? And like Dominic, she was probably too stiff with cold even to try.

Dominic took a step towards her. 'Are you looking for me?' he asked gently.

'Oh . . . Mr Corde . . .' she began.

'Can I help you?' he asked gently. 'I don't believe we've met.'

'Sybil Towers. No! I was just . . . well . . . just on my way home.' She did not move.

He had heard her name mentioned in the village and knew her to be a widow. 'Perhaps I could walk with you?' he offered. 'Just to make sure you get home safely. It's a terribly cold evening.'

'Well . . . that's very kind of you.' There was an eagerness in her voice. He could barely see her face under the shadow of her hat and the scarf wound around her neck and shoulders, but he thought she might have been smiling.

He crossed the short distance between them and offered her his arm. She took it, pulling at him very slightly to direct him the right way. Walking at her pace was hard. There was no brisk-ness to keep the blood flowing.

'Is there anything I can do for you, Mrs Towers?' he asked, trying to guess why she had seemed to be following him. 'Do you need some wood bringing in? Or coal?' The moment he had said it he wondered if he had been clumsy. Possibly she had none, and that was the real issue.

'Oh, no, thank you,' she said, shaking her head and shivering.

'Really, I have everything. Very kind of you, but a hand not to slip is all I need.' As if to emphasise it she clung to him harder.

He walked in silence for several minutes, still believing that there was something she wanted to ask him if she could work up the courage. He ought to be able to guess it and help her if it was difficult. Surely a good minister would see needs, understand them before they were voiced?

Perhaps she was just lonely. Hardly anyone would say that. Please, Vicar, talk to me, and break the silence I live in. It doesn't matter what I say or think, but please pretend for half an hour that it does. Listen to me, ask me; then when you go again I shall feel better.

Would she spend Christmas alone too, apart from coming to church? He should ask her to tea. But he should invite her once before that too, so the kindness wasn't so obvious. No one wanted to be asked simply for charity's sake.

'Mrs Towers,' he began, 'I hope one day soon when the snow is a little less deep, you will come to tea with us. My wife and I would be delighted to make your acquaintance better. Possibly you could tell us much about the village, its history, and the people who have lived here. Would you?'

'Oh!' She sounded thoroughly startled. 'Oh, well!' She gripped his arm as if she were in very real danger of falling. 'That would be very nice, I'm sure. When the weather is better, I should be very pleased to come. When there isn't so much snow, you know. Thank you so much. I am nearly home now. Just around the corner.' She pulled her arm away. 'Do have a nice evening. Good night, Vicar. Thank you for your kindness. So nice to see you.' She doubled her speed and disappeared into the gloom, swallowed by the shadows of trees and garden hedges until she was indistinguishable from the other shapes in the night.

There was no point in standing here as if she might change her mind and come back. And yet Dominic had been certain that she had wished to say something more to him. Had he put her off by speaking? He had only asked her to tea, at some time in the future.

Did she already know that Mr Wynter was dead, or did she perhaps fear it? Had he confided in her? Or perhaps living alone with little to do, and with no relatives nearby, she watched and listened in the village. It would not be snooping, just the instinct of a lonely person with time on their hands, but she might have seen or deduced all kinds of things for herself.

He should have asked her. Could she even be in danger herself?

He was freezing in the bone-deep cold. He was beginning to shake now that he had stopped moving. He turned and began to walk back across the snow towards the spires of the church, black against the first stars. He knew the vicarage lay to the right of it, invisible in the trees, its lights kept to a minimum for economy's sake.

When he opened the front door, the warmth engulfed him, and after a moment he smelled the hot pastry, oil lamps, coal, and lavender furniture polish.

'Clarice!' he called out eagerly. 'Clarice?'

She was there a moment later, hugging him. Then she gasped when the ice on his coat touched her neck and throat, before ignoring it and holding him tighter.

After supper, they sat by the fire opposite each other. Outside, the wind rose, whipping the branches, and now and then clattering small twigs against the glass. He told her about speaking with Peter Connaught.

'Did he tell you anything useful?' she asked, leaning forward, eyes intent upon his.

'I don't think so,' he admitted.

She caught his hesitation. 'You think, you aren't sure?'

He looked at her face with its large, tender eyes and vulnerable mouth. Had he brought her into the presence of murder again, into the violence and tragedy of human hatred? He remembered how much she had been hurt the last time, and how afraid he had been himself. She had never doubted him, no matter what the facts had appeared to be. He owed her honesty, but he also owed her protection. He did not wish her to be hurt, ever. And yet if he shut her out, he was alone. He could not tell her half-truths without destroying the thread between them that was so infinitely precious.

'It wasn't what he said so much as a look in his face,' he said, feeling ridiculous.

'He believed you!' she said, understanding instantly. 'You told him Mr Wynter was murdered, and he knew you were right!'

He felt a warmth inside deeper than anything the fire or the room could give him. 'He believes someone has a secret, and that Mr Wynter could have learned it,' he said in confirmation. Should he tell her the rest: the impression in his mind only barely formed?

She was waiting for him to finish. She had something urgent to say also. He could see it in her eyes, in the clenching of her hands in her lap.

'I think he was almost relieved,' he said. 'As if he had feared it, and now that it had happened it could be faced, and he was no longer alone.'

'He isn't alone,' she said quickly. 'And I told John and Genevieve Boscombe as well. I couldn't help it. Dr Fitzpatrick may be furious, but I couldn't ask their help, and lie to them. They wouldn't have helped me anyway, because I had no sensible explanation for what I'd done.'

He was confused, then touched by a tendril of fear, just a tiny thing, but unmistakable. 'What have you done?'

She blinked with guilt, lowering her eyes.

'I wasn't accusing you!' He leaned far forward enough to grasp her hand. 'Clarice! I only meant . . .' What had he meant? He gulped, and then clenched his teeth. 'I was afraid for you. If someone in this village really lured Mr Wynter to the cellar steps and then hit him so hard he died as a result, then it would be foolish to think we are safe if we go looking for the secret that provoked them to it. In spite of the snow and the peace, the kindness, Christmas in a few days, there is still something very terrible here. Just because we haven't lived here all our lives doesn't mean we are safe from it. We have made ourselves part of whatever it is. I'm sorry!'

She took his hand, closing her fingers around it. 'Don't be. The only way to be safe is not to be alone at all. I shall be very careful.'

'No you won't!' he contradicted her sharply. 'I know you! You'll go charging in, doing whatever you think is right. Safety, or anything to do with sense, will be the last thing on your mind!'

She sidestepped the issue. 'I looked at the books,' she told him. 'Very carefully.'

He was confused. 'What books?'

'The ledgers!' she said impatiently. 'The accounts!'

'Oh. Why? I'm sure we can manage until the bishop makes a decision.' He heard the unhappiness in his own voice. He had not meant to allow himself to care so much, certainly not to let Clarice know. But he wanted to belong here, have his own church, his own congregation to teach, to care for, and to learn from. Already he dreaded going back to Mr Spindlewood and his grey, sanctimonious ways, his tediousness of spirit.

'The accounts are not right!' Clarice said firmly. 'There are inconsistencies in the last six months or more.' Her voice was low and tense, and she was staring at him, demanding his attention. 'Someone was stealing tiny amounts from the church collections. Just pennies quite often, never more than a shilling or two. Mr Wynter was putting the amount back from his own money. His own ledgers were balanced to the farthing, except for those amounts. If you look carefully, they tally up.'

He frowned, trying to understand. 'Why?'

'I don't know, and neither does John Boscombe, but there is something bigger behind it, something they really care about. Mr Wynter was hiding it for a reason. John Boscombe didn't say so, exactly, but I saw the moment in his face when he knew it. I will be careful, Dominic, I promise, but we have to find out what it is. How could we stay here and just pretend this hasn't happened, or that we don't know? We do know!'

'But maybe . . .' he stopped.

Her look was withering. 'If there really is a God – and I can't bear to believe that there isn't, in spite of anything Mr Darwin said – then He knows that we know. In the end that's all that counts, isn't it?' Now she needed an answer, not just to that question, but all that was wrapped within it, for all of their lives.

Dominic closed his eyes for a second, two seconds, and three. She had a way of smashing through pretence that left one nowhere to hide. 'Yes, of course that's all there is,' he answered her. 'We must find the truth and deal with it. But please be careful, Clarice. Whoever it is has a secret, which to them is so terrible they will kill a priest to keep it. It could be anything – even another death we don't yet know of. Or something that to us seems trivial, but to them is so grave that they cannot bear it. If anything happened to you, it would be unbearable to me. I love you so much I don't know how I would be any use without you, to myself or to others. I might once have worked alone quite well, but not since I've known you. I've known something too good to forget.'

She smiled, but her eyes were full of tears. 'I'll be careful,' she promised, sniffing and blinking hard. 'I'm much too happy to let anyone take it away from me either.'

The morning was bright, with a cold, hard wind. They had been in Cottisham little over a week. It seemed for longer. Clearing away breakfast dishes and wondering if Mrs Wellbeloved would come today or not, Clarice felt as if it were months ago that she and Dominic had first walked into this comfortable hallway and she had been so immediately at home. There had been not the slightest shadow of tragedy then. The whole vicarage had been warm with the memories of generations of families living here. They would have had their joys and griefs like everyone, but a security of faith in this small community, under the shadow of the church and the sound of its bells.

How could she have imagined that below there, in the darkness of the cellar, the vicar himself was lying alone, growing colder and colder each day? Would it ever get really warm again? Not until they had found the truth and faced it.

Dominic had gone to see Dr Fitzpatrick. It was not a duty he was looking forward to, but there were many issues to be dealt with. The village must be told officially of Mr Wynter's death. No doubt most people had heard already. Dominic would have to remain silent while the doctor passed off the cause of death as natural. He had written to inform the bishop, of course, but whether the letter had reached him depended on the snow not being too deep for a horse and trap to get out of the village. Even the main roads could be impassable if it had drifted. So far he had received no reply, and he might have to hold the funeral regardless of that.

Clarice stood in the middle of the kitchen floor, towel in her hand, overtaken by surprise by how much she dreaded being replaced here. It would be crushing; a disappointment so powerful it was almost physical, as though someone had bruised her inside. She wanted to stay here, not only because Dominic wanted it so much, but also for herself. In spite of what she had found in the cellar, she wanted to live in this house, see spring come to this garden. She wanted to see the village pond unfrozen, and with the spring ducklings on it, and with their funny little flat feet on the new grass. She wanted to see the apple trees in blossom, and children flying kites. She wanted to be here for Easter, and summer, and Harvest Festival. It could be a fulfilment she had never known before, for both of them. There was good work to be done. Dominic would become as loved as Mr Wynter had been, and she would watch it, and help.

First they must learn who had killed Mr Wynter, and why. They could not find the light if they had not the courage to explore the darkness. Everyone had secrets: it was within the nature of life, whether they were acts of wrong, or merely of foolishness. Guilt and embarrassment could look alike. But which one had provoked murder?

She thought about her visit to the Boscombes yesterday as

she put away the crockery and cleaned the top of the range. She restoked it and then started to warm the flat irons to press Dominic's clean shirts, which were now rolled up damp in the scullery and awaiting her attention.

The Boscombes' was such a happy house, and yet she had sensed a fear there. Or was that too strong a word? Had it been no more than anxiety, and sorrow because a friend had died tragically? She had not imagined the glance between them, so quick as to seem guarded, a communication they preferred not to put into words. Nor had she imagined the small but very clear signs of recent poverty.

What was their sudden misfortune, and had Mr Wynter known about it? She had no idea, but it was very possible. One thing she was certain about, and that was that both John and Genevieve Boscombe were aware that Mr Wynter knew secrets, at least one of which was dangerous. They had understood instantly what the tiny thefts were, and why he had concealed them.

Were they also protecting each other? Why did she ask herself that, when she was perfectly certain that they were?

If Mr Wynter had known some secret about them, what could it be?

She tested the irons on the hob. They were hot enough. She must pay attention to what she was doing. She could not afford to scorch Dominic's shirts. Apart from the fact that she had too much pride in being a good wife careful enough not to damage his clothes, they were far too expensive to replace. They came from the days of his profession as a banker, long before he decided to be a minister.

She kept a piece of extra rag to test the temperature before touching the iron to a shirt. She tried it now, carefully; only when she was satisfied did she begin to iron.

If the vicar had known something about the Boscombes, it would have to be something they cared about passionately, and she did not believe that could ever be money. What was the most precious thing in the world to them? Not material goods of any sort. Not power or fame. They had never had either, nor would they want them. They treasured warmth in their home, the laughter of children playing, the certainty of gentleness and companionship, and the good things that all people of true sanity want.

What could jeopardise those things?

The iron was getting hot in her hand. She snatched it off the collar and was flooded with relief that there was no brown mark on its white surface.

Could there be something wrong with the Boscombes' marriage, and somehow the vicar had discovered it? Had Genevieve been underage at the time? She looked several years younger than John. Perhaps her father had not given consent, and they had run away to be married, and lied to obtain permission. Did that make their union illegal? Had she been from a wealthy family, and promised to someone else? But that would not invalidate their marriage.

Were any of their children conceived or born out of wedlock?

That would be scandalous, but not irrevocable. Why would Mr Wynter concern himself with it? It might be a sin in the eyes of the Church, but it was over and done with now. Surely a confession and absolution would deal with it.

She could find out. She had only to go to the church itself, which was next door across the strip of grass and up the path through the graveyard. The church records would be there in the vestry: marriages, christenings, and burials. Boscombe had said Genevieve grew up here. She would have been married here too.

Very carefully she finished the final shirt. She put both irons to cool and carried the shirts upstairs.

Clarice felt rather grubby, searching the parish records for someone else's secrets, but sometimes one could feel grubby doing what was necessary to get to the truth. And if she found she was wrong, so much the better.

She put on her outdoor boots again and her heavy cape, and then picked up the keys and went out. The snow was almost up to her knees in places where the land was low and it had drifted. The bare honeysuckle vine on the lich-gate was sparkling with icicles, and the path through the gravestones was slippery. The sky was ragged now, with patches of hard light making the expanse of the village green difficult to look at, the snow glaring achingly white. She wondered if someone had fed the ducks. She should make sure; take them something herself.

The church was bitterly cold inside. The stained-glass window with its pictures of Christ walking on the water cast patches of blue and green and gold light on the floor. The robe of St Peter in the boat was the only warm colour: a splash of wine. How many people down the centuries had brought their joys and their griefs here, made promises, prayed for forgiveness, or poured out their thanks?

She hurried to where the parish record books were kept. She unlocked the cupboard, using a key on a labelled hook in the vestry, and found the one most likely to contain the baptism of the Boscombes' oldest child. She skimmed through a couple of years worth of entries before finding it. It was a swift job, since the village was small: just four or five hundred people. Then she started to go backwards, looking for John and Genevieve's marriage. She went through ten years, and did not find it. Twenty-three years before the birth of their first child, she came across Genevieve's own baptism. Even more carefully she moved forward. There were baptisms of two sisters of Genevieve, then the burial of both her parents. The sisters' marriages were recorded, but not baptisms of any children. Presumably they had moved to wherever their husbands lived.

Then Genevieve's children were baptised, but Clarice could find no reference to her marriage.

Of course they could have been married somewhere else, but the ugly thought kept intruding into Clarice's mind that perhaps they had not been married at all. Why would that be? The only reason she could think of was that something had prevented it. The obvious thing would be that one of them was already married. If it were Genevieve, the whole village would probably know, therefore it must be John.

Had Mr Wynter somehow found that out?

She closed the book and replaced it, locking the cupboard door. She walked back through the icy vestry and outside into the freezing world again. It glittered sharp on daggers of water from the earlier thaw, now hanging from every black branch.

Her feet crunched on the surface. There were grey clouds looming in from the west, fat-bellied with more snow. Little shivers of wind stirred the topmost branches.

When Dominic returned at lunchtime, Clarice told him what she had found.

'She could have been married somewhere else,' he said, taking a fresh piece of bread and another slice of cold mutton. 'Perhaps in his village. He might have had elderly parents who couldn't travel, for example.'

She passed him the rich, sharp pickle. 'Possibly. But the Boscombes are in some kind of hardship. There are lots of small signs of it, if you look.'

He smiled with a touch of sadness, and she saw the mounting pain in his eyes. They were not in that situation themselves, but it was not too far ahead of them if he remained a curate much longer. She regretted having said it, yet she could not deny the evidence she had seen in the Boscombes' house. Perhaps avoiding the subject of poverty was in a way making it worse, as if it were a secret too shameful to acknowledge.

'People do fall on harder times without there being a dark secret,' he pointed out ruefully.

'I know.' She poured him more tea although he had not asked for it. One of her pleasures was to notice his habits and meet them before he said anything. 'It's just a little piece of information. But I think it fits in with the missing pennies in the ledgers, the fact that John Boscombe suddenly resigned from his position in the Church, and that they are both afraid of something. None of which would matter if Mr Wynter were not dead. But he is, and it is our responsibility to find out the truth and pursue some sort of justice. At least for now, this is your village.' Then she corrected herself. 'Our village.'

He frowned. 'Why would their not being married, and the vicar knowing that, have anything to do with financial hard times, or the petty thefts from the collection? That doesn't make any sense.'

She struggled through the confusion in her own mind. 'I think he knew about the petty thefts before giving up his job keeping the books. He was close enough to the vicar that they trusted each other. Then something happened, and John Boscombe left. They still go to church, as everyone does, but that's all. Could mean their sudden tightening of circumstances dates from that time too. With children you can go through sheets quickly. You'll wash them every other week, perhaps give them a little rubbing. Middles can wear thin. Best to trim them before they actually tear.'

'Every other week?'

She smiled. 'Two pairs each,' she said gently. 'One on the bed, one in the laundry. It takes two or three days to wash, dry and iron things.'

He coloured faintly. 'Yes, of course.'

'And they have four children,' she went on. 'Things probably get passed down. They may already have been pretty worn six months ago.'

'And what caused the hardship?' he asked. 'Mr Wynter was blackmailing them, so they paid for half a year, and then they killed him?'

She blinked. 'No! No, I don't believe that. But maybe if Mr Wynter found out, so did someone else. That's possible, isn't it?'

Dominic considered for a moment, staring at his cup, but without reaching for it. 'Yes,' he said finally. 'Who would that be?'

'His first wife,' she said without hesitation. 'Or, really, his only wife.'

'Why didn't she come forward and accuse him openly, if he deserted her?'

'Oh, Dominic!' she said in exasperation. 'Don't be so over-worldly. Much better to ask him for money to keep quiet about it than admit to everyone that he ran away from her to be with someone else. Except that if Genevieve doesn't know, or didn't at the time, then he probably ran away just because she was ghastly.'

He tried to hide a smile, and failed. 'Clarice, you don't just run away because your husband or wife is appalling, or there would hardly be a married person in England living at home.'

She raised her eyebrows very high. 'Thank you. I hadn't thought of running away . . . yet.'

He shook his head. He was learning to tell the difference between her teasing and when she was genuinely confused or hurt. 'I'm so glad,' he said drily. 'It's cold out there. Do you really think the Boscombes have a secret?'

She wrinkled her nose. 'Yes. And I think it could have to do with their marriage. That is the only thing of sufficient importance to them that they might fight very hard to protect it.' She met his eyes and hoped he could see in hers that she understood the Boscombes perfectly. She too would have fought with every weapon she had to protect her marriage. For her, too, it was the most precious thing she had.

He reached across the table and touched her fingertips gently. 'I agree,' he answered. 'And I am beginning to think that Sir Peter Connaught also has something about which he is less than honest.'

She was startled. 'Sir Peter? Are you sure? You don't think he's just . . . grieved? He seemed to be very fond of Mr Wynter, and they never made up their quarrel before he died. That makes people feel very guilty, you know.'

He fiddled with his knife. 'I thought of that, but it's more a matter of little things that don't fit: discrepancies in his stories about his parents. Perhaps they don't even matter, but I noticed them.' He seemed about to add something further, and then changed his mind. He looked unhappy.

'What is it?' she asked. 'What are you thinking?'

He gave a slight shrug. 'I don't know. People do boast sometimes, exaggerate their abilities, or money, all sorts of things.

But Sir Peter doesn't seem in any need to do that. He is obviously a man of great wealth, or he could not maintain a place like the manor house. And it is superbly kept. He gives generously to the village; I know that from Mr Wynter's remarks in his notes. And the whole Connaught family is above reproach. Their history is pretty well public.'

'They could still have secrets,' Clarice pointed out. 'Almost every family does.' She bit her lip. 'We certainly do, for heaven's sake. I would go to great lengths to prevent anyone in Cottisham knowing about my mother.' She felt hot with shame even saying it to Dominic, who already knew everything about it. It was he her mother had become obsessed with, convinced she was equally in love with him, and he had very nearly been blamed for murder. Clarice knew what secrets could cost and what length people could be driven to by love, and fear. 'Dominic, it is possible the Connaughts also have something they would pay a great deal to keep unknown,' she went on. 'It is very hard to live with people prying through your affairs. Perhaps that was at the root of Sir Peter's quarrel with Mr Wynter. They used to be close; in fact they played chess twice a week.'

Dominic looked at her unhappily. 'Mr Wynter quarrelled with Peter Connaught and with John Boscombe. Are you saying that he was behind some kind of extortion, or threat of exposure?'

'I don't know. Sometimes "the wicked flee when no man pursueth". Maybe just his knowledge was enough.'

He said what they were both thinking. 'Or he used his special knowledge in the most appalling betrayal imaginable:

to blackmail those who had trusted him, and even turned to him for help, and forgiveness?'

Clarice gripped his hand across the table. 'We didn't know him,' she said urgently. 'Perhaps we have imagined him the way we wanted him to be.'

'Everyone speaks well of him,' he pointed out, closing his fingers over hers.

'Well they would!' she said, biting her lip. 'He was a priest, and he was away temporarily. Who is going to say he was brutal, a slimy betrayer of trust who blackmails the most vulnerable? They would only know it if they had been a victim themselves, and wished him dead, possibly murdered. Who would admit that?'

'No one,' he said miserably. 'Please God, I hope you're wrong. We're wrong,' he corrected himself.

Dominic went out again to visit one of the old gentlemen who was too frail to leave his house in the snow, and afraid of what the deepening winter would bring.

He stayed a little while, assuring Mr Riddington of his care. Regardless of who the vicar of Cottisham should be, he would always have time for going to those who could not come to the church. Then after bidding him goodbye, he walked along the lane towards the green. Again he became aware of footsteps behind him. They seemed to be gaining on him, as though the person were keen to catch him up.

He stopped and turned. He saw the brisk figure of Mrs Paget

hurrying towards him, her breath white vapour in the freezing air.

'I'm glad to see you, Mr Corde,' she said warmly as she reached him. 'Have you been to see Mr Riddington? Poor old soul can't make it even to his front gate any more. Afraid of slipping and breaking a leg. Very wise he stay in. Broken bone at his age can be very nasty. Don't let me hold you up. I'll walk beside you.' Without waiting she started forward again, and he was left to keep step with her.

'Mrs Blount next door drops in every day,' he told her.

'Not the same as having the vicar call.' Mrs Paget shook her head. 'No one else can comfort with the spiritual promises of the Church.'

'Believe me, Mrs Blount is a far better cook than I am,' he replied. 'And there are times when a hot apple pie is more use than a sermon.'

'You may joke, Vicar,' she said seriously, 'but there are dark things to fight against, darker than most folk are willing to admit.'

He was uncertain how to answer her. The wind was rising again. It whined in the branches above them, and little flurries of dry snow skittered over the ice.

'I know the truth,' she went on, her voice quiet but very clear. 'Mr Wynter was murdered, wasn't he? Please don't try to spare me by denying it. It doesn't help to close one's eyes. That's how evil flourishes – because we want to be kind, and end up being cruel.'

He wanted to argue, but she was right. He asked her the question that filled his mind. 'How do you know that, Mrs Paget?'

Now it was she who was silent. They were out of the lane and starting across the open green. The pond was almost invisible: just a smooth white surface a little lower than the slope of the grass. The air was darkening, colour staining the west with fire and the shadows growing so dense the houses blended into one another. He began to think she was not going to answer.

'Mr Wynter was here in Cottisham over thirty years,' she said at last. 'He knew a lot about people, sometimes things they'd rather no one did. He wouldn't have told, of course. Priests don't, do they?' It was not really a question, but she stopped, as if waiting for him to speak, her features indistinguishable in the shadows.

'No,' he replied. Was she trying to find a way to tell him that Mr Wynter had done infinitely worse than use his privileged knowledge to manipulate and extort? The darkness felt as if it were inside him as well as beyond in the sky and the black ice of the trees.

'But those that betray don't trust anyone,' she said, looking straight ahead of her.

'Is that why you believe he was murdered, Mrs Paget?' Dominic asked. 'Just that he knew people's secrets? All priests do.'

'What are most village secrets?' she asked. 'A few silly mistakes, a little spite. All things you can repent of.' Suddenly her voice dropped and became bitter. 'Cottisham's different. But here there are things that are against the law of God and a priest can't overlook, or forgive them.'

'God can forgive all sins, Mrs Paget,' he pointed out.

'After you've paid,' she said harshly. 'Not while you're still committing them, and the innocent are suffering. Don't tell me that's God's way, 'cos it isn't. I know that, and so do you, Vicar.'

'Yes,' he said a little tartly. 'And Mr Wynter would have pointed that out to anyone who was continuing to do what was wrong.'

'Exactly,' she agreed, staring at him. 'But what if that person didn't want to stop? What if they weren't going to stop, no matter what?'

He did not want to know, but he could not avoid it simply because it was uncomfortable. If a priest refused to address sin, what use was he to anyone? He was here precisely to deal with weakness: physical or spiritual. He must face it, wherever it led him.

'What you say is true, Mrs Paget. But I imagine you expect me to do more than agree in theory?'

'You didn't know Mr Wynter,' she said after another few steps. The emotion was carefully controlled in her voice now, and he could not see her face. 'He was a good man. He was brave and honest. He knew right from wrong, and he didn't flinch from doing what he had to, even though he didn't like it.'

'Did he know things about more than one person?' he asked. He was trying to evade the issue and he knew it. Perhaps she did too.

'He might have known things about a lot of people,' she admitted. 'But he knew that John and Genevieve Boscombe are living together in sin. He walked out on his first wife. Left her alone to fend for herself. Vicar never told a word, but I don't come from Cottisham, and I know one or two other places as well. I recognised him.'

'And told Mr Wynter?' he asked.

'No I didn't,' she said stiffly. 'But if I had, I'd have been doing those poor children a service.'

'Branding them as illegitimate?' he said, disbelief making his voice hard. 'The scandal would ruin the parents and make them all outcasts. How is that a service, Mrs Paget?'

'Only if the vicar told people,' she answered with exaggerated patience. 'And he wouldn't do that. You said so yourself.' There was triumph in her, but thin and shivery, full of hurt.

'You haven't been a vicar very long, have you?' she observed.

Dominic felt the heat burn up inside him, in spite of the ice edge of the wind. 'No. What do you suppose Mr Wynter intended to do?' He wanted to know for himself, but also because it might lead him towards whoever had killed Wynter.

'Face them,' she said simply. 'Tell them they have to put things right. Go back and face Mrs Boscombe, the real one, and care for her, make some restitution for what he's done. Perhaps if he's lucky, she'll divorce him for his adultery with her that calls herself his wife now. If all that happens, then they can marry and make their children legitimate at last, by adoption or however it's done. Not their fault, poor little souls.'

He felt an intense pity, more than she could have understood. His own first marriage had been less than happy, as he understood happiness now. He had not left his wife, but he had certainly betrayed her more than once. She may well have expected it, but that excused nothing. He still had a guilt to expiate, and he knew and accepted it. That certain knowledge made him far quicker to forgive others, to understand ugliness and stupidity and try to heal it rather than destroy the perpetrator.

'You are quite right,' he said to her gently. 'That would be the correct thing to do, even if not the easiest.'

'He never lacked courage.' She kept walking at a steady, even pace. 'Takes courage to be a priest, Mr Corde. Can't just go around being nice to people. Sometimes that isn't the real help.'

'Yes, Mrs Paget. I'm sure it isn't,' he agreed.

'I'm home now. Good night, Vicar.'

'Mrs Paget!' he said quickly. 'You said Mr Wynter knew things about many people.'

'So he did,' she cut across him. 'But it's no good asking me what things they were, or who they were about, because I don't know. I just knew that one because I knew. I've lived in other villages too. Good night, Vicar.' This time she turned and walked away briskly up the path.

'Good night, Mrs Paget,' he said more to himself than to her.

It was not a good night. He knew that after supper he would have to go and see John Boscombe, and ask him if what he had been told was the truth, because that was what Mr Wynter was doing before he died. He had racked his brains to find another alternative, all the time knowing that there was none. Clarice had offered to come with him, and he had refused. She had no part in it and no chaperone was necessary. She would worry, he knew that, imagining all kinds of anger and distress, but that was the burden of a priest's wife, and she did not ask to be relieved of it.

It was a hard walk to the Boscombes' house. His arm ached from carrying the lantern and trying to hold it against the wind.

He was welcomed in. The house was warm, although not as warm as the vicarage where they could afford to burn a little more coal.

'How nice to see you, Mr Corde,' Boscombe said immediately. 'It's a terrible night for visiting. What brings you? No one ill or needing help?'

Dominic almost changed his mind. Maybe this was something the bishop should deal with, or whoever was given this living permanently. But if he evaded it now, Clarice would despise him. He could imagine her disappointment in him.

He followed Boscombe inside to the parlour where Genevieve was sitting sewing. She was patching the sleeves of a jacket. She put it away quickly as if to welcome him, but he saw from the quick flush in her face that she was ashamed. Were they really paying blackmail to someone? Had they paid the vicar? Please God, no.

Or to anyone else, perhaps from Boscombe's home village?

Even Mrs Paget? But it was Mr Wynter who was dead. Mrs Paget was very much alive.

'Genny, please get the vicar a cup of tea, or soup,' Boscombe requested. 'Which would you like?'

How could Dominic accept the man's hospitality, given out of their little, with what he had come to say? Guilt almost choked him. And who was he to blame a man for doing what he might so easily have done himself, had the temptation been there? However, Sarah was dead, and he was free to love Clarice as he wished, but due to luck, not virtue.

'No thank you, not yet,' he prevaricated. 'But I would like to speak to you confidentially, Mr Boscombe. I beg your pardon for that, on such an evening.'

'Don't worry, Vicar,' Genevieve said quickly. 'I have jobs to do in the kitchen. You just call when you'd like the soup.'

'What is it?' Boscombe asked as soon as the door was closed and they were alone. 'You look very grave, Vicar. Not more money gone, is it? Or did you find out who took it? I think Mr Wynter was inclined to let it go, you know. He could always see the greater picture, the one that mattered.'

'Yes, I imagine he could,' Dominic answered. 'It seems to me he thought past today's embarrassment and saw the grief that could come in the future if present sins, however easy to understand, or even to sympathise with, were not put right.'

Boscombe's face paled and his eyes were steady on Dominic's face.

'I'm sorry,' Dominic said gently. 'There is no record of your marriage in this parish. If I ask the bishop, will he find it in some other place?'

Boscombe's voice was husky, his eyes wretched. 'No, Vicar. Genevieve is the wife of my heart, but not of the law. Mr Wynter knew that, and he wanted to find a way for us to make it right, but I couldn't stay on within office in the Church once he knew.'

'But you could stay until that?' Then, the moment the words were out of his lips, Dominic wished he had not said them. It was a criticism Boscombe did not need, however justified.

Boscombe blushed and looked down at his big hands. 'I wasn't the one who told him. I couldn't bring myself to. I wanted to be happy,' he said softly. 'That was the coward's way, I suppose, but he asked me to help with the money and other tasks in the church. I couldn't refuse without telling him why.' He twisted his fingers together, crushing the flesh till they were white. 'I didn't think you'd find out so quick.'

'Did you kill Mr Wynter?'

Boscombe's head jerked up, his eyes wide. 'No! God in heaven, man, how can you ask such a thing? He was my friend! He wanted us to put it right, and I told him I wasn't leaving Genevieve for anything, Church or no Church. And I wasn't going back to my first wife either. If God sent me to hell, at least I'd have a life first. But go back and it would be hell now. And who would support Genny and my children?'

'Who supports your first wife?' Dominic asked.

'She had money of her own and no need of mine,' Boscombe said bitterly. 'As she often reminded me.'

'If she divorced you for your adultery and desertion, you would be free to marry Genevieve, and make your children legitimate,' Dominic pointed out. 'In the law, if not in the Church. Wouldn't it still be better?'

Boscombe gave a sharp bark of laughter. 'Do you think I didn't ask her to? She's not a woman to forgive, Mr Corde. Not ever. As long as she lives she'll hold me to bondage. My only choice is to live in sin with Genevieve, the best and gentlest, most loyal woman I know, or live in virtue cold as ice with a woman who hates me, and will make me pay every day and night of my life, because I don't love her. Mr Wynter wanted me to make it right, for Genevieve's sake, and my children's. He told me they'd get nothing if I die, and I know that's true.' He blinked several times. 'I'll just have to pray I don't die. He was looking for a way for me to make it right with God, but he never found it before he died. I don't know who killed him, but I swear to you before the Lord who made the earth and everything in it, that it was not me. I loved Mr Wynter, and I've got enough on my soul as it is without adding violence to it.'

Dominic believed him. It fitted with what Mrs Paget had told him, and what he had come to know of Wynter. Boscombe might have thought, in a moment's desperation, that if Wynter were dead he could continue to live in peace. But he must have known that it would only be a matter of time before he was exposed. With murder on his hands and his heart, there would be no happiness ahead for him, or for the woman and the children he loved so deeply. Could Dominic find an answer for him? If

Wynter, with a lifetime in the Church could not, then how could he, a novice?

'I'll try to find a way for you to sort it out,' he promised rashly. 'Thank you for your honesty.'

'If there were, we'd have found it by now,' Boscombe said miserably. 'What are you going to say to the bishop?'

'Nothing,' Dominic replied, again rashly. He stood up. 'I'm concerned with finding who killed Mr Wynter. Anything else is between you and God. Living with a woman to whom you are not married may be a sin, but it is not against the law. We will address that problem later. Perhaps after Christmas they will move me somewhere else. I hope not, but I cannot choose.' He heard the roughness of grief in his own voice and was angry with himself. What had he to grieve over, when he was returning to the woman he loved, with no shadow over them or between them, except whatever he might create himself by being less than she believed of him? 'First let us celebrate the birth of Christ, and leave other things until after that.'

Boscombe held out his hand, blinking rapidly again 'Thank you.'

Dominic gripped him hard. 'But if I stay here, we will have to seek an answer, one day.'

'I know,' Boscombe replied. 'I know.'

Christmas Eve dawned bright. The sky was a pale, wind-scoured blue, and the ice crust on the snow was almost hard enough to support a child's weight. Certainly the few ducks out, eager for bread, paddled across the tip of it without even making it crack. Someone had been thoughtful enough to put out water for them, but it would need thawing every hour or two.

Clarice had baked fresh bread, a skill she was very proud of because it had not come naturally to her. Dominic took a loaf to old Mr Riddington, and found him frail and hunched up in his chair. He was grateful for the bread, but even more for the company in his chilly and almost soundless world. Dominic brought in more wood and coal, and made them each a cup of tea. He found it was over two hours before he could decently leave the old man.

He went next door to check with Mrs Blount, and thank her for her kindness. Then he set out home.

He was close to the green again when he was aware of footsteps behind him. He heard every crack and crunch of the ice. He turned to see Sybil Towers struggling to catch up with him. Her hands were waggling awkwardly to keep her balance, her cape was trailing lopsidedly and her hat was a trifle awry.

It was the last thing he wanted to do, but he started back towards her. She looked so frantic and lonely he had no choice.

'Good morning, Mrs Towers. Are you all right?' He offered her his arm. 'It isn't weather for hurrying, you know. Where are you going? Perhaps I can accompany you and see you don't fall.'

'You are too kind, Mr Corde.' She grasped his arm as if it had been a lifebelt in a stormy sea. 'Those poor ducks. I know Mrs Jones is putting out bread and a little lard for them, such a nice woman.'

'Which way are you going, Mrs Towers?' he asked again.

'Oh, over there.' She gestured vaguely with her free arm, and nearly lost her balance again. 'How are you settling in? Is Mrs Corde finding the vicarage to her liking? A home matters so much, I always think.'

'We both like it very much indeed,' he answered.

'A good garden,' she went on. 'Old trees make a garden, don't you agree?'

'Yes,' he nodded. 'I expect in spring they are beautiful.'

She told him how many blossom trees there were, then the various other flowers in season, all the way through to the tawny chrysanthemums and the purple Michaelmas daisies, and the offer of an excellent recipe for crab apple jelly. 'One of my favourites, I confess,' she said with enthusiasm. 'I prefer the tart to the very sweet, don't you?'

They were now well across the green and into the lane at the far side. They had passed several cottages and the way through the woods lay ahead, winding between the trees. Presumably it led eventually to open fields and perhaps a farm or two. Dominic had realised half a mile ago that she was not actually going anywhere. She needed to talk to him, but could not bring herself to come to the subject easily. His hands were numb and his feet were so cold he was losing sensation in them also, but he felt her need as sharply as the wind rattling the bare branches above them. Did she know something about Mr Wynter's death and that was what she was struggling to say?

'Of course we will probably not be here for very long,' he

prompted her, surprised again by the regret in his voice. 'Once the bishop finds a permanent replacement for Mr Wynter, we will return to London. From everything I hear, he was a most remarkable man, one whose shoes it will not be easy to fill.'

'He was,' she said eagerly. 'Oh, he was. So kind. So very patient. One knew one could trust him with anything.' She took a deep, shuddering breath. 'But I think perhaps you are the same, Mr Corde. It seems to me you are a man who has understood pain.' She looked away from him, and he knew she was afraid she had been too bold.

He hastened to reassure her. 'Thank you. That is a very fine thing to say, Mrs Towers. I shall endeavour to live up to it. At least I can say that I understand loneliness, and the grief of knowing that you have done something ugly and wrong. But I also know that there is a path back.'

They walked in silence for several yards. Crows wheeled up in the sky, cawing harshly, then circled back into the lower branches again.

'I was going to speak to Mr Wynter,' she said at last. 'I wanted to make a confession, but . . .'

'I think he knew that,' Dominic said for her, stopping walking as well, but still holding her arm. 'Let's turn back, or we will have too far to go. All the earth is God's house. You do not have to speak in a church for it to be a sacred trust.'

'No, no, I suppose not. I kept doing little things wrong, you see, to find out if he would forgive them, before I . . . before I told him the real thing.'

He walked a few moments, perhaps thirty or forty yards along the path, and then he prompted her again. 'Was it you who took the pennies from the collection for the poor?'

She drew in her breath with a little cry. 'It was only pennies! I made it up, always! I gave extra . . .'

He put his other hand over her arm, holding her more tightly. 'That doesn't matter. The books were never short. I know that. But you wanted to speak to him, and never quite found the resolve.' He did not use the word 'courage'. 'Perhaps now would be a good time?'

She gulped again. 'I . . . I committed a . . . a terrible sin when I was young. I'm so ashamed, and it can never be undone. I wanted to confess, but . . . but I . . . he was such a good man, I was afraid he would despise me . . .'

'Then tell me, Mrs Towers. I am not so very good. I understand very well what it feels like to sin, and to repent.'

'I do repent, I do!'

'Then cast it on the Lord, and be free of it.'

'But I must pay!'

'I think that is not for you to decide. What is it you did that is so heavy for you to bear?'

'I had a love affair,' she whispered. 'Oh, I did love him. You see I am not Mrs Towers. I never married. And . . . and . . .' Again she could not find the words.

He guessed. 'You had a child?'

She nodded. 'Yes.' She took a few more steps. 'I only saw her for a few moments, then they took her away from me. She was so beautiful.' The tears were flowing down her face now. In moments the wind would freeze them on her cold skin. She must have been nearly seventy, and yet the memory was as sharp as yesterday.

He ached to do anything that would take away the pain. Could the compassion in his own heart speak for God? Surely God had to be better, greater than he was?

'Is that all?' he asked her.

'Is that not enough?' she said incredulously.

'Yes. And the penance you have already paid is enough also. More than enough. God forgave you long ago. And Mr Wynter would have told you that, were he here.'

'I wish I had had the courage to tell him,' she said, swallowing hard.

'Did he not guess?' he asked.

'Oh, no. He knew I wished to say something, but he did not know what it was.' She sounded certain.

'He knew many people's secrets,' he went on. They were now almost back to the far side of the village green. 'Do you not think perhaps the father could have told him?'

'Oh no, indeed not. The father . . . never knew. It would have been quite impossible for him to marry me. There was no purpose in my telling him about it. I simply went away. It is what girls do, you know.'

'Yes, yes. I do know.' He did not say any more. It was an age-old story of love and pain and sometimes betrayal, sometimes simple tragedy. It had happened untold times, and would happen again. Had it been here in this village? Peter Connaught's father, even, a man of birth and heritage who would never have been permitted to marry a village girl, and one who was not even a virgin at the altar? The fact that it was his child would be irrelevant.

She had protected him all these years. She would not betray him now, and it was not part of her penance that she should.

Dominic was still holding her arm, and he gripped it a little more tightly as they stepped into the rutted road, icy where wheels had pressed the snow down, deep between.

'Thank you for speaking to me,' he said sincerely. 'Please don't think of it any further, except with love, or grief, but never again with guilt.'

She nodded, unable even to attempt words.

He left her at her door, and turned to walk back towards the vicarage. He was quite certain that he had said to her exactly what Mr Wynter would have, and his admiration for the old man's wisdom and compassion grew even greater.

How would Dominic make himself follow in his footsteps and guide and comfort the people of this village, be strong for them, judge wisely, know the hearts and not merely the words?

He would be here for Christmas – that much he was certain of. What could he say that was passionate and honest and caught the glory of what Christmas was truly about? It was God's greatest gift to the world, but how could he make them see that? There would be yule logs and carols and bells, mulled wine, gifts, decorated trees, lights across the snow. They were the outer marks of joy; how could he make just as visible the inward ones as well?

He wanted Clarice to be proud of him; he wanted it with a hunger close to starvation. He must give her the gift she most wanted too – finding the best in himself for both of them.

Of course, he said nothing to her of what Sybil Towers had told him, and he found that a hardship. He would have liked her advice, but he never considered breaking the trust.

Instead, over luncheon, Clarice told him that Mrs Wellbeloved had been in, in the morning, brought yet more onions and another rock-hard cabbage, which with a strong wrist and a sharp knife she could slice well. The two together with mashed potato, gently fried and crisped, made a delicious dish, normally known as 'bubble and squeak'. Mrs Wellbeloved was buzzing with gossip about poor Mr Wynter's death, and the fact that John Boscombe had had a terrible quarrel with him shortly before. The village was full of it, but no one had the faintest idea what it was about.

'His marriage, or lack of it, I should think,' Dominic replied. Since it was Clarice who had discovered it, that was not a confidence between the two of them. 'Poor man.'

'You sympathise with him?' Clarice said in surprise.

'Don't you?'

'I do with Genevieve, if she didn't know. Very little if she did,' Clarice responded.

He smiled. 'If I had been married unhappily, and met you, I might have done the same.'

'Oh.' She did not know whether to smile, or disapprove. She tried both, with singular lack of success.

He saw the conflict in her face and laughed.

'And you think I would have lived with you anyway,' she said hotly. She took a deep breath and speared a carrot with her fork. 'You're probably right.'

He smiled more widely, with a little flutter of warmth inside him, but he was wise enough not to answer.

At almost two o'clock he set out to go up to the manor. There were one or two favours he wished to ask Peter Connaught with regard to villagers he knew were in need, but more than that, he wondered if perhaps Peter's father could have been Sybil Towers' lover. If Mr Wynter had known that, was it a secret worth killing him for? Did it even matter now, so many years afterwards? It would be a scandal, and Peter was inordinately proud of his family and its heritage of honour and care in the village. It was not his fault, of course, but the stain would touch him because he was the one here. Was he protective enough of his father's name to have killed to keep it safe?

What if Sybil's daughter were known to him? She was illegitimate and had no possible claim in law, even if her heritage could be proved – which it probably could not. But in a small community like Cottisham, proof was irrelevant; reputation was all.

The weather had deteriorated. The wind was rising. Clouds

piled high in the west, darkened the sky, promising deep falls of snow that night.

Dominic was welcomed at the hall, as always, and in the huge withdrawing room the usual log fire was blazing. The afternoon was dark and the candelabra were lit, making the room almost festively bright.

He accepted the offer of tea, longing to thaw his hands on the warm cup as much as looking forward to the drink. They addressed the business of the village. Help must be given with discretion; even the most needy do not like to feel they are objects of charity. Many would rather freeze or go hungry than accept pity. Food could be given to all, so none was singled out. They would arrange for the blacksmith to go after dark and add a few dozen logs to certain people's woodpiles.

The butler came with tea, and hot toasted teacakes thick with currants and covered with melted butter. The two men left not a crumb.

Finally Dominic had to approach the subject of Sybil Towers. He had thought about it, considered all possibilities, and found no answer that pleased him fully, but he could not break Sybil's confidence.

'I have to ask you a very troubling question,' he began. He was awkward. He knew it, and could think of no way to help himself. 'I have gained certain knowledge, not because I sought it, and I cannot reveal any more to you than that, so please do not ask me.'

Peter frowned. 'You may trust my discretion. What is it that is wrong?'

114

Dominic had already concocted the lie carefully, but it still troubled him. 'Many years ago a young woman in the village had a love affair with a man it was impossible for her to marry. There was a child. I believe the father never knew.' He was watching Peter's face but he saw nothing in it but sympathy and a certain resignation. No doubt he had heard similar stories many times before.

'I'm sorry,' Peter said quietly. 'If it happened long ago, why do you raise it now?'

'Because Mr Wynter may have known of it,' Dominic said frankly, still watching Peter's face. 'And he was murdered.'

'Are you absolutely sure of that?' Peter demanded, his voice hoarse. 'You thought it might be an accident the other day, and murder is very far from what Fitzpatrick told me!'

'I know. Dr Fitzpatrick does not want to face the unpleasantness of such a thing. But I believe Mr Wynter was a fine man, and his death should not be treated with less than honesty, just for our convenience. He deserved better than that.'

'What makes you think it was murder, Corde?' Peter reached for the poker, readjusting his grasp on it, and drove the end into the burning embers. The log shifted weight and settled lower, sending up a shower of sparks. He replaced the poker in its stand and added another log.

Dominic found himself shivering in spite of the heat. 'He fell at the bottom of the cellar stairs,' he replied. 'There were marks of being dragged, and he was found in the second cellar, with injuries both to his face and the back of his head. The cellar door was closed behind him, and he had no lantern.'

There was silence in the room. Beyond the thick curtains and the glass, even the sound of the wind was muffled.

'I see,' Peter said at last, his face sombre in the firelight. 'I have to agree with you. As an accident that does not make sense. How tragic. He was a good man: wise, brave and honest. What is it you think this unfortunate woman has to do with it? Surely you are not suggesting Mr Wynter was the father of this child? That I do not believe. If he had done such a thing – which of course is possible; we are all capable of love and hate – then he would have admitted it. He would not have lied or disclaimed his responsibility.'

'No,' Dominic agreed. 'But I think he may have known something of the truth, and someone could not bear the thought that he would reveal it. Perhaps he even wished them to honour their responsibility in some way they were not prepared to.'

'How very sad. What is it I can do to help now? I presume you will not tell me the names of either the woman or her child?'

'I will not tell you the name of the woman,' Dominic agreed. 'It has to be confidential. The name of the child I do not know, but I fear it may be someone who has returned to the village with a certain degree of retribution in her mind.'

'Oh dear! And killed poor Wynter because he was the vicar at the time, and did not do as she would have wished, or thought fair?'

'It seems possible,' Dominic replied. That at least was true.

The more he considered it, the more likely it became. The missing money and Wynter's quarrel with John Boscombe had already been explained.

Peter was waiting for an answer to his first question.

'You must be very careful,' Dominic said softly. 'If it is this woman who kills, then she does it with stealth, and skill. I think it may be someone nobody suspects.'

'Why should she wish me any harm?' Peter's eyes widened. 'Forty years ago I was a child myself. In fact I was not even in England. That is when my parents were living in the East, before . . . before my mother died.' He looked down and a faint colour touched his cheeks.

'Did your father not return to England at all during that time?' Dominic asked.

Peter looked up sharply. The whole air of their conversation had altered. There was pain in his face, and anger. His body was stiff in the chair. 'Exactly what is it you are asking, Corde?'

'She could not marry him because he was far beyond her social station,' Dominic told him. 'It seems in Cottisham that a man of that status is most likely to have been your father.'

Peter's face paled to a sickly yellow, as if the blood had drained out of his skin. He was shaking when he spoke. 'My father was devoted to my mother! It is monstrous that you should make such a revolting suggestion! Who is this woman? I demand to know who has . . . no . . . I apologise. I know you are bound not to tell me.' His hands gripped the arms of his chair. 'But she is a liar of the most vile sort. It is not true!'

Dominic was startled by the vehemence of his denial. It was not so very unusual that a man of wealth and position should produce a few illegitimate children. It made Dominic wonder if perhaps Peter himself might have quarrelled with Mr Wynter over it. Was it conceivable that, charming as he was, generous, diligent in his duties, still his family pride was such that he would have struck out in rage at the suggestion that his father had begotten any child other than himself?

'You seem inexplicably angry at the thought, Sir Peter,' Dominic said gently. 'It does not threaten either your inheritance or your title, and it is no more than a remote possibility. I told you, in case you yourself were in some danger. Your flash of temper makes one wonder if perhaps this same suggestion was the cause of your difference with Mr Wynter, and you did not forgive him for making it.'

Peter stared at him, and slowly the awful meaning of what he had said dawned on him. 'God in heaven, man! Are you saying you think I murdered poor Wynter because he believed it was true my father begot this . . . this child? You can't!' He dragged in his breath, gulping, painfully, and then he started to laugh. It was a terrible sound, wrenched out of him with pain.

Dominic was appalled. He wanted to run away, leave this scene of naked emotion, but he must stay, find the truth and then face it.

'Is that really absurd?' he said when Peter had gained some small measure of control.

'Yes! Yes, it is absurd!' Peter's voice rose still to near hysteria.

'My father could never have had an illegitimate child. Would to God he could have.'

The words made no sense at all. Yet in the small discrepancies in what Peter had said of his parents a tiny glimmer of light appeared.

'Why would you want that?' Dominic asked.

Peter leaned forward, his face beaded in sweat, eyes dark. 'You know, don't you? Did Wynter leave something that you found? He swore to me he wouldn't, but what is his word worth, eh? What is yours worth, Reverend?'

'Why do you want your father to have begotten an illegitimate child?' Dominic asked again, his voice perfectly steady now. He was still trying to untangle the confused threads in his mind. 'Do you want this woman to be your sister? Do you know who she is? Did she kill Wynter?'

'I've no idea who killed Wynter, or why!' Peter said, forcing the words between his teeth. 'And my father did not beget her. At least Sir Thomas Connaught didn't. He was sterile. God knows who my father was. I don't.'

Dominic was stunned. Was that why Peter was so defensive of his mother, the beautiful woman who had died tragically, somewhere in the East? Had Thomas found out her infidelity, and killed her? No, that was impossible. If he knew he could not have fathered a child, then he would have killed her when he knew she was expecting, not after the child was born. It still made no sense. 'He killed her?' he said, struggling for some kind of logic in it.

119

'You fool!' Peter shouted at him. Then he covered his face with his hands. 'Of course he didn't! He never even knew her. I was an orphan, one of thousands of children who live on the streets. I was good-looking, intelligent. Sir Thomas found me stealing and lied to the police to save me. He had no children, and he knew he never would have. No wife either. He adopted me. I am quite legally and honourably his heir. But I am not of his blood. I am no more a Connaught of Cottisham Hall than you are. I am illegitimate, unwanted. I have no father and no mother that I remember. Either she died, or she gave me away. It hardly matters now. I don't belong here. Wynter knew. That's what we quarrelled over. He wanted me to stop boasting about my heritage.' He lowered his hands slowly. 'I hated him because he knew. But he was my friend, and I would never have harmed him, that I swear on the little honour I have left.'

Dominic spoke slowly, weighing each word. 'Did Mr Wynter not tell you that it was the pride of blood that was wrong? A man is great, or petty, because of who he is, not who his father was. Sir Thomas Connaught gave you the opportunity to be his son and carry on the tradition of service that his father gave to him. If you have done so, then your actions have earned you the right to be here. Respect and the love of the people is earned, it cannot be bequeathed by anyone else.'

'You know your father!' Peter said with a raw edge of pain in his voice, almost of accusation. 'You were part of him, whatever you did. That is a bond you cannot make with all the wishing in the world.'

'You have no idea whether I knew my father or he knew me,' Dominic pointed out. 'Actually I looked like him, so I reminded him of all that he disliked in himself.' The words were still hard to say. 'He greatly preferred my brother, who was fair and mild-featured, like my mother, whom he adored.' He was surprised that he remembered it even now with a sense of exclusion and strange, inexplicable loss.

'I'm sorry,' Peter apologised. 'My arrogance is monumental, isn't it? As if I were the only one in the world who felt he did not belong in his own skin, his own life. You say you know who this woman is, the mother? Perhaps I could do something to help her. You could attend to it, discreetly.'

'It isn't your responsibility,' Dominic pointed out.

'Haven't you just been telling me that that is irrelevant?' Peter asked for the first time smiling very faintly.

'Yes. Yes, I suppose I have,' Dominic agreed. 'You understand me better than I understand myself. By all means, help her. She has little in the way of possessions. Enough to keep her warm would be a great gift.'

'Consider it done. And the others in the village who are in any need. The estate has plenty of wood, and certainly no better use for it.'

'Thank you.' Dominic meant it profoundly. He smiled back. 'Thank you,' he repeated.

While Dominic was at the manor house, Clarice took a lantern and went down into the cellar again. Mrs Wellbeloved had swept the steps, but Clarice knew which one had the splinter on it that had frayed Mr Wynter's trouser leg, and where he must have landed at the bottom.

Carefully she continued on down the steps, holding the lantern high. No one could come down here without a light of some sort, and a candle would be blown out by the draught from the hall above.

But who would Mr Wynter go into the cellar with? What excuse had that person given? To fetch coal for him, on the pretext that it was heavy? No it wasn't, not very. Mrs Wellbeloved normally did it herself. She was strong, but not like a man. And where was the coal scuttle to carry it in?

Whoever it was had dragged Mr Wynter's body from the bottom of the steps across the floor and into the other cellar, leaving the marks in the coal dust. Why? They had tried to scuff them out, but hadn't entirely succeeded. Why make them in the first place? He was an old man, light-boned, frail. Why not carry him?

Because the killer had not been strong enough to carry him. A weak man? Or a woman? Genevieve Boscombe? It was a sickening thought, but Genevieve had much to lose. A woman will do most things to protect her children. A bear, to protect her cubs, will kill without thought, and without guilt.

She turned around slowly and started climbing back up again, glad of the light from the hallway at the top. She reached it and was facing Mrs Paget.

'Sorry to startle you,' Mrs Paget said with a smile. 'I took the liberty of coming in. The door was unlocked; Mr Wynter always left it unlocked too. And it's bitter outside. That wind is cruel.'

'Yes of course.' Clarice felt as if she should apologise for being less than welcoming. After all, there was a sense in which the vicarage belonged to the whole village, and Mrs Paget had obliquely reminded her of that. 'Please come in. It's warmer in the kitchen. Would you like a cup of tea?'

'That's very kind of you,' Mrs Paget accepted. 'I brought you a bottle of elderberry wine. I thought it might be pleasant with your Christmas dinner. The vicar was very fond of it.' She held out a bottle with a red ribbon around its neck, the liquid in it shining clear purple.

'How very kind of you,' Clarice accepted. She blew out the flame in the lantern and set it on the hall shelf, then took the bottle. She led the way into the kitchen and pushed the kettle over on to the hob to boil again. Thank goodness today she had cake. She must not get the reputation for having nothing to offer visitors.

Mrs Paget made herself comfortable in one of the kitchen chairs. 'I see you were down in the cellar again,' she remarked. 'Not to get coal.' Her eyes wandered to the full coal and coke scuttles by the stove, then back to Clarice. 'Hard for you, that it happened right here.'

Clarice was taken aback by her frankness. 'Yes.'

'I suppose you're working out what happened?'

Should she deny it? That would be pointless. It was obviously what she had been doing, and Mrs Paget knew it. That too was clear in her eyes.

'Trying to,' Clarice admitted.

'Poor man. That was a terrible thing.' Mrs Paget shook her head. 'But vicars sometimes get to know secrets people can't bear to have told. You be careful, Mrs Corde. There's wickedness in the village in places you wouldn't think to look for it. You watch out for your husband. A pleasant face can very easily fool men. Some look harmless that aren't.'

Clarice decided to be just as blunt.

'Indeed, Mrs Paget.' She thought of the marks of dragging in the cellar floor. The vicar had trusted a woman he should not have, perhaps even trying to help her. 'Do you have anyone in particular in mind?'

Mrs Paget hesitated, but it was clear in the concentration of her expression that she was not offended at being asked.

The kettle started to steam and Clarice warmed the teapot then placed the leaves in and poured on the water, setting it on the table to brew. She sat down opposite Mrs Paget, still waiting for an answer.

Instead Mrs Paget asked another question. 'What did you find down there?'

Clarice was not sure how much she wanted to answer. 'Nothing conclusive.'

Mrs Paget surprised her again. 'No doubt you were disturbed by my coming. I'm sorry about that. I did call out, but not loud enough for you to hear down there. Perhaps there is something, if we looked properly. The poor man deserves justice, and that old fool Fitzpatrick isn't going to do anything about it. I'll come with you, if you like? Hold the lantern.'

Clarice felt her stomach tighten, but she had no possible excuse to refuse. And she could not bring herself to tell Mrs Paget a deliberate lie. For one thing, it could be too easily found out if anyone at all were to go down there, and what could she say? She needed to keep the evidence; it might be the only proof of what had happened. 'Thank you. That would be a good idea. I didn't really have time to look.'

After tea and cake, Clarice went gingerly down the steps again with Mrs Paget behind her, holding the lantern. Of course they found exactly what Clarice had already seen. 'That was where I found him.' She pointed to the doorway of the second cellar.

'So he fell here,' Mrs Paget said quietly, pointing to the bottom of the steps. 'And whoever it was dragged him from there,' she indicated the marks, 'over to there.'

'Yes, I think so.'

Mrs Paget studied the floor. 'By the shoulders, from the look of it. And those are their own footmarks . . . unless they are yours?'

Clarice stared at the distinct mark of a boot well to the side of the tracks. 'It might be Dr Fitzpatrick's,' she said with a frown.

'Going backwards?' Mrs Paget asked gently, her eyes bright. 'Why would he do that, unless he were dragging something? And it looks a little small, don't you think?'

She was absolutely right. It was a woman's boot, or a boy's.

As if reading her thoughts, Mrs Paget said the same thing. 'Tommy Spriggs, one of the village boys, said he saw a woman hurrying away from here the day the vicar was last seen. He'll tell you, if you ask him. Hurrying, she was.'

'Who was it?'

'Ah, that he doesn't know. Could've been any grown woman who could walk rapidly and wasn't either very short or very tall.'

'Can you take me to him?' Clarice asked.

'Of course I can.' Mrs Paget picked up her skirts to climb back up the stairs again. 'Good thing you came down here, Mrs Corde. And a good thing you're not minded to let injustice go by, simply because it's easier and, I dare say, more comfortable.'

In the evening Clarice told Dominic about it, and of finding Tommy Spriggs, who confirmed what Mrs Paget had said.

'Had he any idea who she was?' Dominic asked.

'None at all. What he had told Mrs Paget was all he knew,' she answered. She looked at him, both fearing the same answer. Neither spoke it.

By early afternoon it was so cold the windows were blind with fresh snow, and even inside the air numbed fingers and toes. Outside all colour was drowned; white earth, white sky. Even the black trees were mantled in white. Just a few filigree branches were hung with icicles here and there, though when it had thawed sufficiently for them to melt into daggers of ice was hard to say.

Blizzards blew in from the east, and through that cold-gripped world Genevieve Boscombe came to the door and asked to see Dominic.

The study fire was not lit, so he took her into the sitting room. He spent several moments poking the wood and coal until the fire caught a better hold and started to give a little more heat. Only when she sat down and he looked more closely at her eyes did he realise that no hearth in the world was going to assuage the cold inside her.

'I killed Mr Wynter,' she said quietly. Her voice was flat, almost without emotion. 'He was going to tell everyone, so all the village would know. I couldn't take that, not for my children.'

Dominic was stunned. After what Clarice had told him the previous evening they both knew it was horribly possible that Genevieve Boscombe was guilty. Even so, he could not easily believe it. He hated the thought. He liked both of them. But then how good was he really at judging character any more deeply than the superficial qualities of humour or gentleness, good manners, the ability to see what was beautiful? And he sympathised with her. He understood those who truly loved and could not bear to lose the warmth and purpose from their lives.

'I did!' she repeated, as if he had not heard her. 'It's not a religious confession, Vicar. I expect you to tell the police so they can arrest me.' She sat with her back straight and her hands folded in her lap. Her eyes were red-rimmed, but there were no tears in them now. He thought she had probably done all her weeping, at least for the time being.

'How did you do it, Mrs Boscombe?' he asked, still reluctant to accept and looking for a way for her to be not totally at fault.

She looked surprised, although it was visible as just a momentary flicker of the eyes. 'I carried the coal scuttle down for him,' she replied. 'I hit him with it. He fell, and I pulled him into the other cellar, so he wouldn't be found too soon.'

'But you knew he would be found some time,' he said.

'I didn't think. I don't remember.' And she refused to say anything further, merely requesting that he report her to the constable so she could be arrested.

There was, in effect, no constable, only the blacksmith, who was appointed to represent the law in the village. She insisted in going with him. After much protest, the blacksmith locked her in the large, warm storeroom next to the forge.

Dominic went straight to tell John Boscombe what had happened, trudging through the snow. He was cold inside and out, even when he stood in Boscombe's kitchen in front of him.

'She only said it to protect me!' Boscombe said frantically. His face was haggard, his eyes wild. 'Where is she? I'll reason with her. I was the one who killed the vicar. I quarrelled with him because he wanted me to get straight with the law and the Church.' His voice was rising in pitch, rising desperately. 'I had an accident in the summer. Could have been killed. Was then the vicar told me that if I had been, my family would get nothing, not even the house, because they weren't legal. Genny and the children would be thrown on to charity, and folks might not be that kind to them, seeing I still had a wife alive that I'd never sorted things with.'

'I see,' Dominic said quietly. 'And did you believe that Mr Wynter would have forced you to do this, whatever the cost to you?'

Boscombe hesitated.

'Did you?' Dominic insisted.

'I was afraid he would.' Boscombe evaded a direct answer. His eyes were angry, challenging. 'That's why I did it. Genny's innocent. She didn't even know I was already married when she . . .' He stopped.

'Agreed to live with you without marriage?' Dominic asked.

Boscombe was caught. To deny it would suggest Genevieve did not care about marriage, and that was obviously ridiculous.

'Was the vicar blackmailing you?' Dominic asked.

'Good God, no!' Boscombe was appalled, but a tide of colour swept up his face.

Dominic guessed the reason.

'Then who is?' he said. 'I don't believe you killed Mr Wynter, nor did Genevieve. But you are each afraid that the other did, so there must be a terrible reason why it could be so. Someone is threatening you. Who is it?'

Boscombe's face was wretched – eyes full of shame.

'My wife. She's here in Cottisham. She's asking for money every week. She'll bleed us dry.'

All the jumbled pieces were beginning to make sense at last.

'But she's still alive, isn't she?' Dominic said gently. 'Why would you kill Mr Wynter, and not her? Why would either of you?'

Slowly the darkness melted from Boscombe's face and he straightened his shoulders, leaning forward a little as if to rise. 'It wasn't Genevieve! It was Maribelle! The vicar wouldn't have forced us to do the right thing, only helped us, but if we did, then Maribelle would get nothing! And he knew what she was doing! He wanted it all out, just like you did!'

'Maribelle?' Dominic asked, although by now he was certain he knew. His blood chilled at the thought of her alone with Clarice in the cellar where she had killed Mr Wynter, but there was no time to stare into nightmares now.

'Maribelle Paget was my first wife,' Boscombe admitted. 'And a crueller woman never trod the earth.'

'Come.' Dominic stood up. 'We must go and face her.'

'But Genevieve!'

'She's safe. We have other things to do first. She thinks you did it, and she won't back down from her confession until we've proved otherwise.'

After Dominic had left with Genevieve Boscombe, Clarice stood in the kitchen staring out of the window at the snow on the apple tree, going over and over in her mind what Mrs Paget had said in the cellar. The impression would not leave her that Mrs Paget expected to find the footprint where it was, almost as if she had known it was there. She had read the drag marks without hesitation, knowing what they were. How did she do that so accurately? Why did she assume that the woman seen leaving the vicarage in the wind and snow had had anything to do with the vicar's death? She could have been anyone.

The way she had described the murder accounted for there being no broken glass. She had even known at which step he had fallen. She had stopped at it instinctively.

Clarice turned from the window, went into the hall and tore her cape off the hook, wound it around herself, and set off in the snow towards the Boscombes' house. She must tell Dominic immediately that neither John nor Genevieve was guilty. She was afraid John Boscombe might panic, even fight Dominic when he heard what had happened, and do something that in itself would condemn him.

Clarice took the shortcut along the path through the trees. The stream would be frozen over and easy to cross. The Boscombes' house was only just beyond.

The crust of ice was hard. For a moment it bore her weight, then cracked and pitched her off balance. The knife-edged wind sighed in the branches, blowing clumps of heavy snow on to the ground. Two or three fell close to her, distracting her attention. She was almost upon the three figures before she saw them, dark and blurred in the colourless landscape. It was Dominic and John Boscombe facing Mrs Paget.

Clarice stopped abruptly. The stream was to her right, identifiable only as a winding strip of level ground between the banks.

They must all have seen her, but it was Mrs Paget, ten feet closer, who moved first. She plunged forward through the deep snow, flailing with her arms, crossing the ground with extraordinary speed. She reached Clarice in moments, her face contorted with fury.

Clarice stepped back, but not quickly enough. Mrs Paget grasped hold of her, fingers like a vice, pulling her towards the stream, dragging her along. She had no time to think. She struggled, but her fists struck only heavy cloak.

Dominic was shouting something, but another avalanche from above drowned his words. The snow was melting.

Now they were on the stream and it was easier to move; there were no thickets of waterside plants to trap them.

'It won't hold you!' Mrs Paget shouted, triumph loud and high in her voice. 'Step on to it and we'll all go down!' She turned her voice to Clarice. 'Struggle too hard and you'll crack the ice under us, clever vicar's wife! Believe me, the cold under there will kill you!'

Clarice stopped moving instantly.

'Good,' Mrs Paget said with satisfaction. 'Now come with me, slowly, carefully. When we get to the far side, I might let you go. And then I might not. They're too heavy to come after us. Nothing they can do.' She pulled again hard and Clarice almost overbalanced.

Boscombe and Dominic stopped at the brink, knowing their weight would break the ice.

Mrs Paget laughed, with a high, vicious sound. She yanked on Clarice's arm and started forward again. Clarice did all she could to resist, but her feet had no purchase on the ice. She heard it before she realised what it was: a sharp sound, like a shot, then a tearing as of ripping cotton.

Mrs Paget screamed, grabbing at Clarice and holding on to her hand so hard Clarice cried out in pain. Mrs Paget was on her back, legs thrashing. The ice swayed and tipped, the cracks in it fanning out, the black water swirling over it, as cold as death, her big cloak imprisoning her in its folds.

Clarice felt the water with a shock that almost took the air from her lungs. The cold was unbelievable. She could not even cry out.

Dominic started out across the ice, calling her, heedless of the danger to himself. Boscombe was in the shallows, knee deep, then waist deep, his whole body outstretched to hold on to Dominic's arm.

Clarice was paralysed with the cold, her hand still gripped by Mrs Paget's like the jaws of a trap, hard as steel.

Dominic took her other hand, pulling, but Mrs Paget would not let go. If she drowned, Clarice would drown too.

Dominic reached past her. There was a piece of branch in his hand. He swung and struck hard, catching Mrs Paget's fingers with a force enough to break the bone. She shrieked once, drawing the black water into her lungs, and then she was gone.

Dominic and Boscombe dragged Clarice out. She was almost unconscious, and shuddering so violently she could barely breathe. She saw lights in the gloom and heard voices. She drifted into a kind of sleep.

She woke with someone rubbing her hands and arms, then her legs. Someone else put hot tea between her lips, and she swallowed it awkwardly. It hit her stomach like fire and made her choke.

Then she saw Dominic, his face white with fear.

'Don't be so silly,' she whispered hoarsely. 'I'm not going to drown. I was just . . . detecting . . .'

He laughed, but there were tears in his eyes and on his cheeks.

'Of course you were,' he agreed. 'You have to hear my Christmas sermon.'

There were murmurs of assent, and more tea, and then it all faded into a blur, distant and happy and full of kindness.

The usual Watch Night service was not held, in deference to the death of Maribelle Paget. However, word rapidly spread of exactly how it had come about, if not why. Nor did anyone mention that she was really Maribelle Boscombe.

But in the morning, every man, woman and child was in the village church to celebrate Christmas Day. Even old Mr Riddington was there, wrapped in a blanket and fed liberal doses of blackberry wine.

The bells rang out over the snow, carrying the message of

joy across fields and woodlands, from spire to spire throughout the land. Inside the organ played the old favourites, and the voices sang – for once in total unison.

Dominic went to the pulpit and spoke simply, passionately, knowing that what he said was true.

'Christmas is the time when we give gifts, most especially to children. Many have spent long hours making them, carefully and with love, putting the best into them that they have. There are dolls, toy trains, a wooden whistle, a new dress, painted bricks.'

He saw nods and smiles.

He leaned forward over the pulpit rail. 'We are the children of God, every one of us, and nearly nineteen hundred years ago He gave us the greatest of all the gifts he has, greater even than life. He gave us hope: a way back from every mistake we have made, no matter how small or how large, how ugly or how incredibly stupid, or how shameful. There is no corner of hell secret enough or deep enough for there to be no path back, if we are willing to climb back up. It may be hard, and steep, but there is light ahead, and freedom.'

Deliberately he did not look at Sybil Towers, or at Peter Connaught, nor did he look at the Boscombes with their children, nor Mrs Wellbeloved nor Mr Riddington. Only once did he glance at Clarice and saw the pride and the joy in her. It was all the reward he ever wanted.

'Do not deny the gift,' he said. 'Accept it for yourself, and for all others. That is what Christmas is: everlasting hope, a way forward to the best in ourselves and all that we can become.'

'Amen!' the congregation replied. Then again, with passion, they rose to their feet one by one. 'Amen!'

Above them the bells pealed out across the land.

Headline hopes you have enjoyed *A Christmas Secret*, and invites you to sample the beginning of *A Christmas Beginning*, another novel by Anne Perry, also available from Headline.

1

A CHRISTMAS BEGINNING

So this was the Isle of Anglesey. Runcorn stood on the rugged headland and stared across the narrow water of the Menai Strait towards the mountains of Snowdonia and mainland Wales, and he wondered why on earth he had chosen to come here, alone in December. The air was hard, Ice-edged and laden with the salt of the sea. He was a Londoner, used to the rattle of hansom cabs on the cobbles, the gaslamps gleaming in the afternoon dusk. The streets were always busy with the singsong voices of costermongers, the cries of news vendors, driver of every kind of vehicle – from broughams to drays – and the air carried the smell of smoke and manure.

Here must be the loneliest place in Britain, all bare hills and hard, bright water, and silence except for the moan of the wind in the grass. The black skeleton of the Menai Bridge had a certain grace, but it was the elegance of power, not like the low, familiar arches across the Thames. The few lights flickering on in the town of Beaumaris behind him indicated nothing like the vast city he was used to, teeming with the passions, the sorrow, and the dreams of millions.

Of course, the reason he was here was simple: he had nowhere else in particular to be. He lived alone. He knew many people, but they were colleagues rather than friends. He had earned his promotions until he was now, at fifty, a senior superintendent in the Metropolitan Police. But he was not a gentleman, and he would never be that. He had not the polish, the confidence, the ease of speech and grace of movement that comes with not having to care what people thought of you.

He smiled to himself as the wind stung his face. Monk, his colleague of years ago, once even his friend, had not been born a gentleman either, but somehow he had always managed to seem to be one. That used to hurt, but it did not any more. He knew that Monk was human too, and vulnerable. He could make mistakes. And perhaps Runcorn himself was wiser.

The last case in which they had worked together had been difficult and, in the end, ugly. Now Runcorn was tired of the city and he was due several weeks of leave. Why not take it somewhere as different as possible? He would refresh his mind away from the familiar and predictable, take long walks in the open, think deeply, for a change.

The sun was sinking in the south-west, shedding brilliant, burning light over the water. The land was dark as the colour faded and the headlands jutted purple and black out of the sea, only the uplands ribbed pale like crumpled velvet.

How long was winter twilight here? Would he soon find himself lost, unable to see the way back to his lodgings? It was bitterly cold already. His feet were numb from standing. He turned and started to walk towards the east and the darkening sky. What was there to think about? He was good at his job, patient, possibly a little pedestrian. He never had flashes of brilliant intuition, but he got there. He had succeeded far more than any of the other young men who had started when he had. In fact he had surprised himself.

But was he happy?

That was a stupid question, as if happiness were something you could own, and have it for always. He was happy at times, as for example when a case was closed and he knew he had done it well, found a difficult truth and left no doubts to haunt him afterwards, no savage and half-answered questions.

He was happy when he sat down by the fire at the end of a long day, and took the weight off his feet, ate something really good, like a thick-crusted ham and egg pie, or hot sausages with mashed potato. He liked good music, even classical music sometimes, although he would not admit it, in case people laughed at him. And he liked dogs. A good dog always made him smile. Was that enough?

He could only just see the road at his feet now. He thought about the huge bridge behind him, spanning the whole surge and power of the sea. What about the man who built that? Had he been happy? He had certainly created something to marvel at, and change the lives of people far into the future.

Runcorn had untangled a few problems, but had he ever built anything, or did he always use other people's bridges as he travelled – where? No more than home to bed in an unfamiliar lodging house. It was comfortable, he would sleep well, he usually did. Certainly it was warm enough, and Mrs Owen was an agreeable woman, generous in nature.

The next morning was sharp and cold, but a pale sun struggled over the horizon, milky soft through a fine veil of cloud, which Mrs Owen assured him would burn off soon. The frost was only a dusting of white here and there, enough to make the hollows stand out on. the long uneven lawn down to the big yew tree.

Runcorn ate a hearty breakfast, talked with her for a little while because it was only civil to appear interested as she told him about some of the local places and customs. Afterwards he set out to walk again.

This time he went uphill, climbing steadily until nearly midday, when he turned and gazed up at a sky naked of clouds, and a sea shimmering unbroken into the distance.

He stood there for some time, lost in the enormity of it, then gradually descended. He was on the outskirts of Beaumaris again when he turned a corner in the road and came face to face with a tall, slender man of unusual elegance, even in his heavy, winter coat and hat. He was in his mid-thirties, handsome, clean-shaven. They both stopped, staring at each other. The man blinked, uncertain except knowing that Runcorn's face was familiar.

Runcorn knew him instantly, as if it had been only a week ago they had met. But it was longer than that, much longer. The case had been one of suicide suspected to be a murder. John Barclay had lived in a house backing on to the mews where the body had been found. It was not Barclay whom Runcorn remembered with affection, but his widowed sister, Melisande Ewart. Even standing here in the middle of this bright, windy road, Runcorn could see her face as clearly as if it were she who were here now, not her arrogant, unhelpful brother.

'Excuse me,' Barclay said tensely, stepping around Runcorn as if they had been strangers, and walking on up the road, lengthening his stride as he went. But Runcorn had seen the recognition in his face, and the distaste.

Was Melisande here too? If she were, he might see her. Even a glimpse. Did she look the same? Was the curve of her hair as soft, the way she smiled, and the sadness in her that had haunted him ever since?

It was ridiculous for him to think of her still. If she remembered him at all, it would be as a policeman determined to do his job regardless of fear or favour, but with possibly a modicum of kindness. It was her courage, her defiance of Barclay in identifying the corpse and taking the witness stand that had closed the case. Runcorn had always wondered how much that had cost her afterwards in Barclay's displeasure. There had been nothing he could do to help her.

He began walking again, round the bend in the road and past the first house of the village. Was she staying here also? He quickened his step without realising it. The sun was bright, the frost nothing more than sparkling drops in the grass.

How could he find out if she was here, without being absurd? He could hardly ask, as if they were social acquaintances. He was a policeman who had investigated a death. It would be pointless to see her, and ridiculously painful. He was a fool even to think of it, and he despised himself.

He hurried on towards his lodgings, the safety of Mrs Owen's dining-room table and the cheerful conversation of strangers.

But he did not stop thinking of Melisande. The weather grew a little milder, well above freezing. He saw more than a hundred birds pecking over a field, and the farmer told him they were redwings. There was plenty of yellow gorse in bloom, and the occasional hellebore in gardens. He walked in the sun and the wind, once or twice in the rain, and over a couple more days learned his way about the shore to east and west of Beaumaris. He found favourite places, hollows out of the wind, the first sign of snowdrops that caught his breath with sudden pleasure, intimate rock pools where strange shells and seaweeds grew.

On Sunday he dressed in the one decent suit he had brought with him and went to the morning service at the church nearest to the place in the road where he had encountered John Barclay. It was a solid stone building with stained-glass windows and a bell that rang out in the gusty air, the rich sound carrying across the town and into the fields beyond.

Runcorn knew why he was here, driven as if by the pull of

a magnet. It had nothing to do with the worship of God, even though he entered through the great carved wooden doors with head bowed, hat in his hand and a mixture of reverence and hope making his heart beat faster.

It was hushed inside, an old church with stone floor and high ceiling crossed with great carved hammer beams. The light was hazy. Colours in the great windows showed the stations of the cross, and what looked like a woman following after the figure of Christ in the street. She kneeled to touch his robe, and Runcorn remembered a story of healing. He could not recall anything more except that there was something beautiful just beyond his reach.

The congregation was already seated and he slipped into a pew towards the side. He watched with interest, bowing his head as Barclay passed by him, then lifting it again with a sudden pang of disappointment that Melisande was not with him. But there was no reason for her to be on this wind-scoured island in its barren glory, its wild coast, its birds, and the roaring sea. What was there here for a beautiful woman to do?

Then another, entirely different woman, perhaps in her mid-twenties, walked past the end of his pew and on up the aisle. She moved with a unique grace, almost fluid, as if she were not touching the hard stone of a church floor with her boots, but were barefoot on grass, or the smooth sand of a beach. Her head was high, and when she turned, her pale face quickened by a secret laughter, as if she understood something no one else did. She was wearing dark green, so sombre it appeared almost black, and her cloud of hair escaped the rather rakish hat she seemed to have put on at the last moment, without thought. Her eyes were peat brown, and wide. Runcorn knew that, even though she looked at him for only an instant.

She went on up to the very front row, and sat down beside a woman perhaps fifteen years older, who greeted her with a quick, warm smile.

Runcorn noticed the movement of a man a couple of rows in front of him because he turned to stare at the girl with an intensity unsuitable in church. He was almost handsome, but for a tightness about his mouth. His features were regular and he had an excellent head of hair, thick with a slightly auburn tone to it. He was perhaps approaching forty.

If the girl were aware of his attention, she showed no sign of it at all; indeed, she seemed indifferent to any of the people around her except the vicar himself, who now appeared. He looked to be in his late forties, or perhaps a little more. He had a pale, ascetic face with a high brow and the same peat-dark eyes as the girl in green. Almost immediately the service commenced, with the usual soothing and familiar ritual. He conducted the proceedings sombrely and somewhat as if it were a habit he was so accustomed to that it required far less than his full attention. Runcorn began to wonder if there were any way in which he could escape the sermon without his boredom being rudely obvious, and concluded that there was not. Instead he would occupy his thoughts by looking at the people.

The man in front of Runcorn was looking at the girl again.

There was too much emotion in his face to believe he was simply admiring her. He had to know her, and there had been conflict between them, at least on his part.

What of her? Runcorn could not see her now because she was facing forward, her attention on the vicar as he began his sermon. His subject was obedience, an easy matter for which to find plenty of reference, but not one so simple to give life or warmth to, or to make relevant to Christmas, now less than three weeks away. Runcorn wondered why on earth he had chosen it: it was singularly inappropriate. But then Runcorn did not know the congregation. There might be all kinds of passions running out of control that obedience could hold in check. The vicar might be the good shepherd trying all he knew to lead wayward sheep to safe pasture.

Barclay was also looking at the girl in green, and for a moment there was a hunger in his face that was quite unmistakable. Runcorn was almost embarrassed to have seen it. Two men courting the same woman? Something that must happen in every village in England.

He had not been paying attention to the service. He had no idea what the curate had risen to do, only that his face was in every way different from that of the vicar. Where the older man was studious and disciplined, this man was mercurial and full of dreams. He seemed barely into his twenties, and yet there was a keen intelligence in him. He looked at the girl in green and smiled, then as if caught in a minor offence, quickly looked away. She turned a little, and Runcorn could see, even in the brief profile of her face, that she was smiling back, not wistfully as a lover, but with life and laughter, as a friend.

He would never know what tangle of emotions bound those people together. He had come because he thought Barclay would be here and, in spite of the absurdity of it, there was a chance he would see Melisande. He would like to think she was happy, whatever it was that had saddened her in London. The thought of her still facing some sort of darkness was so heavy inside him it was tight in his chest, like a physical band preventing him from taking a full breath. Where was she? He could not possibly ask Barclay if she was well. And any answer he gave would be no more than a formality. You did not discuss health or happiness with tradesmen, and he had made it abundantly clear that that was how he regarded Runcorn, and all police: the refuse collectors of society. He had said as much.

The congregation rose again to sing another hymn. The organist was good and the music pealed out with a powerful, joyous melody. Runcorn enjoyed singing. His voice was rich and he knew how to carry a tune.

It was as he sat down again, a moment or two after the people to the left of him, that he saw Melisande. She was nowhere near Barclay, but it was unmistakably her. He could never forget her face, the gentleness in it, the clear eyes, the laughter and the pain so near the surface.

She looked at him now with sudden, wide amazement. She smiled, and then self-consciously turned away.

Runcorn's heart lurched, the room swayed around him and

he sat down in the pew so hard the woman in front turned to glare at him.

Melisande was here! And she remembered him! That smile was far more than just the acknowledgement of a stranger caught staring at her. It was more than civility; it had had warmth. He could feel it burn inside him.

The rest of the service passed by him in a blur of sound, beautiful and meaningless, like the splashes of colour the sunlight painted through the windows.

Afterwards he stood outside in the bright winter stillness as the congregation emerged, talking to each other, shaking the vicar by the hand, milling around exchanging gossip and good wishes.

Someone recognised him as a stranger and invited him to be introduced. He moved forward without thought as to what he was going to say, and found himself shaking the hand of the Reverend Arthur Costain, and offering his name without police rank.

'Welcome to Anglesey, Mr Runcorn,' Costain said with a smile. 'Are you staying with us over Christmas, or perhaps we may hope you will be with us longer?'

In that instant Runcorn made his decision. Melisande and Barclay already knew his profession, but he would tell no one else. He was not ashamed of it, but knowledge that he was a policeman made many people uncomfortable, and their defence was to avoid him.

'I will stay as long as I can,' he replied. 'Certainly until the New Year.'

Costain seemed pleased. 'Excellent. Perhaps you will call at the vicarage some time. My wife and I would be delighted to make your better acquaintance.' He indicated the woman beside him, and with whom the girl in green had sat during the service. Closer to, she was more interesting than his first glance had suggested. She was nothing like as beautiful as the younger woman, but there was a strength in her face that was unusual, full of both humour and sadness. Runcorn found it instantly pleasing, and accepted the invitation, only then realising that the vicar, at least, had said it as a matter of form. Runcorn blushed at his own foolishness.

It was Mrs Costain who rescued him. 'Forgive my husband, Mr Runcorn. He is always hoping for new parishioners. We shall not press you into staying beyond your pleasure, I assure you. Is this your first visit to the island?'

He recognised her kindness with surprise. He was not used to such acceptance from people of her social class. He had lost his sense of where Melisande was in the crowd, but he knew precisely where Barclay was standing, only yards away, looking at him with distaste. How long would it be before he told Mrs Costain that Runcorn was a policeman?

But Barclay was not looking at Runcorn. He was staring at the girl in green, his eyes intent on her face so Runcorn wondered how she was not aware of it, even uncomfortable. There was a brooding emotion in him that seemed both longing and anger, and when the man with auburn hair, who had also watched her, approached, his face tight and bitter, for an instant the tension between her and Barclay was so palpable that others were momentarily uncomfortable as well.

'Morning, Newbridge.' Barclay's voice was curt.

'Morning, Barclay,' the auburn-haired man replied. 'Pleasant weather.'

Everyone else was silent.

'I doubt it will last,' Barclay responded.

'Do you imagine we will have a white Christmas?' Costain put in quickly.

Barclay's eyebrows rose. 'White?' he said sarcastically, as if the word held a dozen other, more pungent meanings. 'Hardly.'

The girl in green swung round to look at him with amusement and then a sudden little shiver, hunching her shoulders as though she were cold, although she was well dressed and there was no wind.

'Olivia?' Costain said anxiously.

'Don't fuss,' his wife's voice was soft. Had Runcorn not been standing so close he would not have heard her.

Costain was disconcerted. He looked from one to the other of them and did not know how to address the deeper meaning that was understood between them.

Barclay nodded curtly and walked over towards Melisande, waiting for him on the path by the lich-gate. Runcorn watched him, and for a moment his eyes met Melisande's and he was unaware of anyone else. Newbridge brushed past him, said something to Olivia and she replied, her voice cool and light. Her words were courteous, her face almost empty of expression. She did not like him; Runcorn was certain of it in that instant.

He thanked Mrs Costain for her kindness, glanced briefly at the others in acknowledgement, then excused himself and went in the opposite direction. He made his way across the grave-yard between the carved angels and the funeral urns and the headstones, and into the shadow of the yew trees beyond. He walked out of the further gate into the road, his mind still whirling.

It was his profession to watch people and read reactions. There was so much more to investigate than the words given in answer. It was as much the way they were said, the hesitations, the angle of the head, the movement and the stillness that told him of the passions beneath. That small group in the church-yard had been torn by emotions too powerful to control except with intense effort. The air was heavy, tingling on the skin like that before the breaking of a storm.

Did everybody else know it too, or was it just he? In spite of his separateness, his observation of the situation so intellec-tually cool, he was as much a victim as any of them. He was just as human, as vulnerable and every bit as absurd. What could be more ridiculous than the way he felt about Melisande, a woman to whom he could never be more than a public servant she had been able to assist, because it was the right thing and she had had the courage to do so, in spite of her brother's disap-proval?

He went back to Mrs Owen's house because he knew she

had cooked Sunday dinner for him and it would be a graceless thing not to return and eat it, in spite of the fact he felt already as if the comfortable walls of the house would close him in almost unbearably. And the last thing he wanted was trivial conversation, no matter how well meant. But he was a man of habit, and he had learned painfully the cost of bad manners.

He had an excuse to leave quickly: the weather was exceptionally pleasant for December, and he determined to walk as far as he could and still return by dusk. The wild, lonely paths along the shore, with the turbulent noise of breaking water and screaming gulls, fitted his mood perfectly. It was nature eternal and far beyond man's control. It was an escape to become part of it, simply by hearing the sounds, feeling the wind in his face and looking at the limitless horizon. It was big enough, and that comforted him. He saw in it a kind of truth.

The next day he walked the shore all the way from Beaumaris, north and east to Penmon Point. He stood and stared at the lighthouse and Puffin Island beyond. The day after he went all the way past the Menai Bridge until he could see the great towers of Caernarfon Castle on the opposite shore, and the vast, white-crowned peaks of Snowdonia. The following day he did the same, walking until he was exhausted.

Even so, he no longer slept well. The next morning he rose early, shaved and dressed, and went outside into the winter dawn. The air had a hard edge of ice on it, so sharp he gasped as he breathed it in. But he found a perverse pleasure in it also. It was clean and bitter, and he imagined he could see the distances it had blown across, the dark, glimmering water and the starlight.

Without realising it he had walked uphill towards the church again. Its tower loomed massive against the paling sky. He went in through the lich-gate and up the path, then round through the graveyard, picking his way across the grass crisp with frost. The dawn was sending up pale shafts of light in the east and throwing shadows from the gravestones and the occasional marble angel.

Perhaps that was why he was almost on the body before he realised what it was. She was lying at the base of a carved cross, her white gown crisp with hoarfrost, her face stiff, her black hair in a cloud around her like shadow. Only the blood drenching the lower half of her body was flooding scarlet with the strengthening daylight.

Runcorn was too horrified to move. He stood staring at her as if he had seen an apparition and if he waited his vision would clear and it would vanish. But the cold moved into his bones, the fingers of light crept around further, and she remained as terribly real. He knew who she was. Olivia Costain, the girl in green who had walked up the aisle of the church as if on a grassy lea.